"DROP THEM GUNS OR I'LL SHOOT!"

Some folks just couldn't follow simple directions.
The gal they'd been abducting dropped her shapely
rump to the top step with her heels dug in stubbornly
as one of them tried to hang on while the other yelled,
"Oh, shit!" and whirled on the landing with his six-
gun in his hand. So Longarm blew him off the landing to flop ass-over-teakettle down the stairs as limp
as a wet dishrag.

By this time Elvira had kicked the one trying to
lift her dead weight in the shins, and so by the time
Longarm put two hundred grains of lead through the
space he'd been in, he too was thumping down the
stairs, and yelling like hell besides.

D0695698

DON'T MISS THESE
ALL-ACTION WESTERN SERIES
FROM THE BERKLEY PUBLISHING GROUP

THE GUNSMITH by J. R. Roberts
Clint Adams was a legend among lawmen, outlaws, and ladies. They called him . . . the Gunsmith.

LONGARM by Tabor Evans
The popular long-running series about U.S. Deputy Marshal Long—his life, his loves, his fight for justice.

SLOCUM by Jake Logan
Today's longest-running action Western. John Slocum rides a deadly trail of hot blood and cold steel.

BUSHWHACKERS by B. J. Lanagan
An action-packed series by the creators of Longarm! The rousing adventures of the most brutal gang of cutthroats ever assembled—Quantrill's Raiders.

TABOR EVANS

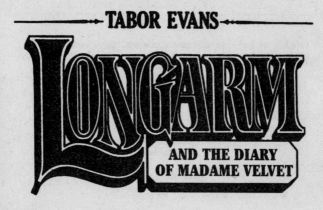

LONGARM

AND THE DIARY
OF MADAME VELVET

JOVE BOOKS, NEW YORK

This is a work of fiction. Names, characters, places, and incidents are either the product of the author's imagination or are used fictitiously, and any resemblance to actual persons, living or dead, business establishments, events or locales is entirely coincidental.

LONGARM AND THE DIARY OF MADAME VELVET

A Jove Book / published by arrangement with
the author

PRINTING HISTORY
Jove edition / October 1999

All rights reserved.
Copyright © 1999 by Penguin Putnam Inc.
This book may not be reproduced in whole or in part,
by mimeograph or any other means, without permission.
For information address: The Berkley Publishing Group,
a division of Penguin Putnam Inc.,
375 Hudson Street, New York, New York 10014.

The Penguin Putnam Inc. World Wide Web site address is
http://www.penguinputnam.com

ISBN: 0-515-12660-8

A JOVE BOOK®
Jove Books are published by The Berkley Publishing Group,
a division of Penguin Putnam Inc.,
375 Hudson Street, New York, New York 10014.
JOVE and the "J" design
are trademarks belonging to Penguin Putnam Inc.

PRINTED IN THE UNITED STATES OF AMERICA

10 9 8 7 6 5 4 3 2 1

Chapter 1

Death came to town in the wee small hours of a raw spring morning, passed by a miner's shack where a sleepless mother hugged her sick baby to her breast, and reined in at a house of ill repute where a late-burning lamp shone through the lace curtains of a top-story window.

The no-longer-young woman seated at a writing table, with that same lamp etching cruel lines across a once-lovely face, never heard Death moving up the stairs, and Death never knocks on any door. The woman felt another pang, and the lamplight seemed to flicker as she dipped her pen again and quietly told the gathering darkness, "I've been expecting you all night, Mr. Death. Have you ridden far?"

Death didn't answer. Mortals couldn't seem to understand Death never ranged all that far away from any of them. The woman shuddered and said, "I'll be with you in a minute, Mr. Death. I just need a few more lines in this diary to leave things nice and tidy."

But as she began to write some more with her right hand, she felt a wave of numbing pain down her left arm and wistfully asked, "Just a minute more, as a professional courtesy, Mr. Death? We both know you owe me for more than one mere mortal I sent to an early grave."

But Death took her then and there, with the pen still

1

gripped in her hand and the last entry in her diary unfinished.

As they were leaving town, Death paused to claim that baby too. For if Death paid any mind to the prayers and tears of mortals, how many mortals would ever die?

The late Madame Velvet had been in the habit of taking her late breakfasts in bed at noon. So they found her slumped over the last volume of her unfinished nineteen-volume diary before her cold flesh could get too disgusting. Everybody knew what you did with the dead body of an old whore. It was all those pages covered with neat spidery handwriting that confused some folks trying to tidy up after her.

So later that same April, the bright morning sunlight was dealing a tad less harshly with the stern but handsome features of one Portia Parkhurst, Attorney at Law, as she paced the landing atop the granite steps of the Denver Federal Building in a severe black woman's suit with a rather silly black hat, with black silk roses growing on it, atop her pinned-up almost-black hair. Portia Parkhurst's hair was *almost* black because, unlike the late Madame Velvet, the lady practicing law in a man's world was inclined to glory in the few silver threads her time before the bar had bestowed upon her. There was nothing she could do but wait for her determined but unlined cameo features to catch up with her prematurely graying locks.

The man she'd been waiting for there was nearly half an hour late. But she'd already heard that U.S. Deputy Marshal Long of the Denver District Court seldom reported for work on time even when it was payday.

In point of fact, she spotted him headed her way at no more than twenty-seven minutes after the hour.

He was easy to spot in a crowd because he strode a head taller than most in his stovepipe cavalry boots. The boots and the coffee-brown Stetson he wore telescoped in a Colorado crush were separated by the tobacco-tweed suit and vest the Hayes Reform Administration inflicted on its civilian federal employees of late. The double-action .44-40 carried cross-draw didn't do much for the drape of his frock coat. But Longarm, as he was better known to friend and foe alike, didn't much care. A man who'd packed a badge for six or eight years tended to have enough foes to require considerable stopping power from a sincere side arm. The double derringer he carried at one end of a gold-washed watch chain across his vest wasn't as noticeable. Like the federal badge he carried pinned to his wallet, it wasn't supposed to be. By the time anyone had forced Longarm to prove he packed a badge or a concealed belly gun, he was likely to feel right irritated with them.

Longarm's gun-muzzle-gray eyes lit up when he spied the trim figure in black hovering at the top of the steps like a pretty little buzzard. He ticked the brim of his hat to the lady lawyer as he joined her on the landing, smiling down at her and causing her heart to skip a beat when she recalled the last time she'd been gazing up at his tanned features and heroic mustache at even closer range, from her pillow. So she said, flustered, "That's not why I'm here. I meant what I said about you and that married woman up on Capitol Hill, you shameless rogue!"

To which Longarm calmly replied, "I plead guily to being no better than I ever said I was, Miss Portia. But fair is fair, and that widow woman I've been consoling up on Sherman Street ain't been married for some time. I never mess with married women. I never mess with *single* gals who throw chinaware at me and tell me never to darken their doors again, as I'm sure you ought to be convinced by now."

Portia sighed and said, "Lord knows I meant it when I hurled that fine Wedgewood creamer at you, Custis Long! But that's not what brings me here this morning. I've helped you with legal advice from time to time, and right now I have a delicate probate problem I need a little help with. Most of my other gentlemen friends are just members

3

of the county courthouse gang, and there's a federal angle I'd like your opinion on.''

It might have been fair, but it wouldn't have been smart to bring up some gossip he'd heard about her and a surrogate judge, a *married* surrogate judge.

He said, ''We'd better let me report in to my office lest I lose my imposing federal position, Miss Portia.''

He escorted her inside. On the way up the stairs he asked who they were talking about. She asked if he'd seen the obituary in the *Rocky Mountain News* on the notorious Madame Velvet, who'd died from a heart stroke out Mulligan way in the nearby Front Range.

He hadn't. But when they came to the oaken door of Marshal Billy Vail's office, Longarm stuck his head in long enough to yell, ''Got a lead on that Mulligan case, Henry!'' and ducked back out to take the bemused Portia Parkhurst by one arm and run as, somewhere behind them, a plaintive voice called back, ''What Mulligan case? The boss said he wanted to see you the minute you came in!''

Longarm whipped Portia around a corner in the marble corridor and explained, ''That was Henry, the squirt we have playing the typewriter in the front office.'' Then he opened another oaken door and hurled her into utter blackness despite the time of day.

He shut the door and bolted it after them as he struck a match to light a fixture on the wall. Its wick needed trimming. The light it shed took ten years off the deliberately mannish appearance Portia affected before the bar. As she gazed around in wonder, she saw they were in a small windowless chamber where a leather chesterfield sofa, a card table, and four bentwood chairs shared such space as there was with floor-to-ceiling file cabinets. As he waved her to a seat on the sofa Longarm explained, ''Used to be nothing but files in here before they moved the Arapaho, Cheyenne, and most of the Ute Nations clean out of Colorado along with a heap of the Bureau of Indian Affairs. None of the powers-that-be around the building ever had any call to come here in person for any files. So a pal from the stenograph pool showed me how they'd fixed it up for playing cards and such when things were slow around here.''

Portia, who prided herself on cross-examining, smiled sweetly and asked, ''What was the stenographer's name and was her game, strip poker? Or did you get right down to business on this chesterfield?''

Longarm tossed his hat on the table, spun a bentwood chair around to straddle it like a pony, and replied, ''Neither one of us is on trial here, Miss Portia. You said you wanted to talk to me about some Velvet Madame in Mulligan. I haven't asked you to talk to me about toad squat since you busted that chinaware on my poor head.''

Portia laughed despite herself and said, ''I hit the doorjamb as you were storming out on me, you big oaf! I never meant half the things I might have said that night, but you made me so mad, sparking that rich widow and me at the same time!''

Longarm shrugged and asked, ''Who was this Madame Velvet? Seems to me I recall old-timers mentioning the name in connection with an earlier day when Denver was still called Cherry Creek and Colorado was still a part of Kansas Territory. Why did they call her Madame Velvet?''

Portia wistfully replied, ''They say she was pretty as a picture and as soft to the touch as velvet when she arrived in the Colorado gold fields less than twenty years ago. I know they struck gold around '58, but the whores and gamblers only arrived with the gold rush of the '60's that helped the Union win the war. They say Madame Velvet was this young widow who'd fallen on hard times and came West to seek fame and fortune. How could she have gone from young and soft to old and tough in such a few short years?''

Longarm suggested, ''The life she seems to have chosen takes more out of a gal than taking in washing or slinging hash, and there's no saying how old her beauty was when she first put it on the market in mighty busy times. I know *I* ain't as soft and velvety as I looked back in West-by-

God-Virginia when nobody had ever heard of Abe Lincoln and our spread still lay in the western hill country of the way bigger state of plain old Virginia. We all get older. Whores and hound dogs get old faster than the rest of us. So this Madame Velvet was better known as a whore back when it was the Union Forever and Pikes Peak or Bust?''

Portia sighed and said, ''So well known, and *popular,* she soon had her own parlor house near the junction of the South Platte and Cherry Creek. It got burned down in the Great Fire of '63. She rebuilt not far below that infamous Larimer Street Bridge.''

Longarm winced and said, ''I was back East, attending this war they were giving at the time. But I've heard the tale from old-timers. So let me guess. Your Madame Velvet had to rebuild again after the Great Flood of '64 lifted the Larimer Street Bridge off it's foundations to tear through a mess of Downstream Denver like a big old blackboard eraser. They tell me the *Rocky Mountain News* wound up way off down the South Platte, stranded on the lone prairie, once the waters went down.''

Portia said, ''Madame Velvet didn't rebuild here in Denver. By then they'd dug into the mother lodes over in the Front Range, and her kind follows boom times as tight as sharks trail a New Bedford whaling ship. So over the years she ran houses of ill repute all up and down the Front Range from Pikes Peak to Fort Collins, with her last few years over in nearby Mulligan, where there seem to be enough hardrock men making a steady three dollars a day to keep her and a modest crew of very modest soiled doves going, now that the bonanza times are but bittersweet memories along the Front Range. But Custis, in her day Madame Velvet was something to see, presiding over Roman orgies that would make a Nero blush, with more than one unsolved killing on or about many a parlor house over the years. Unsolved until now, that is. Madame Velvet was a walking, or should I say horizontal, encyclopedia of Colorado, before and after the war and statehood. She and her girls served hard young toughs who've since gone on to become important men in Colorado business and political circles. A lot of them left some mighty ugly skeletons in more than one whorehouse closet, and wasn't Colorado under federal law before it became a state under Grant in '76?''

Longarm shrugged and said, "Doc Evans was appointed the territorial governor, but ran things sort of locally under his tight Denver political machine. Much the same as New Mexico Territory is being run today. So we don't have any federal warrants out on Billy the Kid and the other survivors of that Lincoln County War. Washington's point in appointing territorial governments is to let somebody *else* run a territory. How did you find out so much about this Madame Velvet's misspent youth in a prewar Colorado neither of us can personally recall, seeing Madame Velvet's dead and can't tell anybody much about it now?''

Portia glanced about as if afraid she'd be overheard as she almost whispered, "That's just it! She *can*! Why she did it I shall never in this world understand, but almost from the day she first sold herself three ways for a dollar in a Cherry Creek crib, the poor disturbed soul kept written business accounts of her sordid business in volume after volume of those leather-bound diaries sold in stationery stores. I've listed nineteen, each covering roughly a year, with some of the early volumes amounting to confessions that could have put her in prison for life had she been lucky. In one entry she as much as tells us right out how she rid herself of a brutal pimp with generous helpings of flypaper syrup over his breakfast waffles. Another entry accuses a man who is now a state senator of beating a girl to death who laughed at his virile member. And there's no statute of limitations on manslaughter!''

Longarm grimaced and said, "If there was, it could still make it sort of hard to get re-elected come November. How did you come by all this inflammatory information, Miss Portia?''

She said, "As the probate attorney retained by the Madame's heirs, two nieces of the deceased who were Kansas spinster shopkeepers and knew next to nothing about their late father's wilder sister. They might have preferred to forget the whole thing when we contacted them, had not a considerable estate been left to them. To their expressed disgust, it seems the wages of sin pay better than selling ladies' notions in Wichita.''

Longarm said, "So I've heard. But what do you expect this child to do about the estate of a dead soiled dove, Miss Portia?"

She said, "One of the spinsters agrees with me that we should burn that nineteen-volume diary and forget we ever peeked. The other wants to show them to a literary agent with a view to publishing an exposé, along the lines of that Mormon girl who claims to have escaped from the harem of Brigham Young."

Longarm made a wry face and said, "Some Mormons I know tell me that book was a big fib, and James Butler Hickok never kissed Calamity Jane neither. So who's to say whether the scribbles of an old bawd are worth anything or not?"

Before she could answer, there came an imperious pounding on the door, and Longarm was glad he'd bolted it when a familiar voice called out, "I know you're in there, Deputy Long! Open the damned door and tell me what you meant about that Mulligan case!"

Longarm put a finger to his lips as Portia stared up at him, wide-eyed as a deer caught in the beam of a jacklight, while out in the hallway, Marshal William Vail of the Denver District Court roared at them, "All right! I'm off to get the damned key, and if I find you in there where I'm sure I'll find you, you can commend your soul to our sweet Lord, for your ass will belong to me!"

Chapter 2

The short and stumpy, but mighty senior and determined, Billy Vail was known around the Federal Building as a man one argued with at one's own peril. So when the janitor Vail dragged up from the basement told the petulant marshal the door wasn't locked, and Vail told him to unlock it anyway, the janitor went through the motions with a passkey in the gutted latch. It was an open secret that the original lock had been replaced with a barrel bolt one locked from the inside to let others know the hidey-hole was in use.

Flinging the unlocked door open, the janitor struck a match to light the fixture Longarm had just snuffed out. Vail stared soberly in at the empty space that still smelled of some woman's perfume as he declared, "I knew the rascal was in here with some gal. So where are they at?"

He turned to the pallid youth he'd left standing by the door while he'd scouted up the janitor and demanded, "Well, Henry? What have you to say for yourself after letting your pal and his doxy slip by you like thieves in the night?"

His clerk-typist indignantly replied, "I never did! They never did! I told him you wanted him back in your own office the moment he came in. I told you what he said about that Mulligan case before I caught just a glimpse of him heading somewhere with a lady in black. That's all I know. If they ever ducked in yonder, as you suspected, they'd still be there. They never came out past *this* child!''

Vail whirled on the janitor to demand, ''Is there another way out? What's behind them file cabinets?''

The man who cleaned the place from time to time, and warned others about those infernal used condoms behind the chesterfield, truthfully told the irate boss, ''Nothing. I helped shift them cabinets in here when they consolidated back files hardly anybody ever looks at. They painted over the one window on the inside. Then we shoved the files in, stacked from floor to within inches of the ceiling, as anyone can plainly see, and that's all there is, there isn't any more.''

Vail measured the narrow gap between the tops of the files and the pressed-tin ceiling by eye. Then he turned to say, ''Henry. You're a tad taller than me. I want you to stand up atop this table and tell us what's hiding in that crawling space.''

The fastidious white-shirted Henry protested, ''There isn't room for anything bigger than a skinny cat to crawl in such space as there may be up yonder, Marshal Vail!''

But Vail insisted. So Henry moved the table over to the files with the janitor's help, and gingerly climbed up on it to peer into the dusty slit and declare with authority, ''I take back what I said about a cat. I make it less than four inches from the solid tops of these files to the ceiling. Have you ever noticed the *size* of your wayward senior deputy, Marshal Vail?''

As the janitor helped Henry down from the unsteady tabletop, Vail asked him, ''Are you sure the backs of these files fit flush against the far wall?''

The janitor started to say something you just didn't say to a boss, took a deep breath, and replied, ''I never measured with a yardstick. We shoved until all the files looked even. You can see they ain't all the same exact size. I told you we'd consolidated back files from a few different offices. But yep, I'd say there couldn't be more than a few inches here and less than a yard's clearance there betwixt them files and the granite wall behind them. There's no way to tell you for certain, because there's no way to get behind them files without we move 'em, and I can tell you true it takes two or more strong men to shift even one of them heavy stacks.''

Vail thought about that. But one of the secrets of command was the avoidance of commands that could carry things all the way to silly. So he kicked a bottom file drawer and decided, ''He must have left the damned building with that pussy after all. Do you reckon he could have really had a lead on that Mulligan case, Henry?''

The pallid Henry shrugged and said, ''I've learned to my sorrow never to bet on Longarm doing one thing or the other, sir.''

So Billy Vail grumped out with Henry in tow. The janitor trimmed the lamp, shut the door, and went through the motions of locking it lest a good thing be lost forever for the working stiffs around the Federal Building.

Behind the filing cabinets, seated in Longarm's lap on the marble sill of the painted-over window, Portia Parkhurst tried to sound less unrefined than she felt when she pouted, ''Left with a pussy indeed! Was that any way to speak in mixed company?''

Longarm said soothingly, ''He didn't know there were ladies present, Miss Portia. What do you suppose he and Henry meant about a Mulligan case? You never told them what you just told me about Madame Velvet, did you?''

She tried to sit up straighter, found it easier to just relax and enjoy the way her trim hips spooned into his lap as they sat there with their feet against the far side of the niche and their knees perforce bent up, and replied, ''I've no idea. You're the only federal employee I've mentioned Madame Velvet's estate to. They may have read her obit in last week's papers. But I'd hardly call it a *case*, Custis. Madame

11

Velvet had been seeing a doctor about her heart trouble for some time, and the county coroner's inquest declared her death no mystery. Can we get down from this windowsill now? It's sort of stuffy back here with the morning sun beating on this painted glass.''

Longarm said, "Not yet. Old Billy used to scout Comanche with the Texas Rangers and he's a sly old dog. What'll you bet he doubles back to see if he can catch us breaking cover?''

She sighed and said, "Help me shed this wool jacket then. I may as well unpin this hat while I'm at it, seeing there's barely light to make one another out back here and . . . Custis, is that an erection I feel down there between my, ah, cheeks?''

He said, "Not yet. But I can't answer for hard feelings against you if you keep wriggling in my lap like so.''

She couldn't resist grinding her tailbone impishly as he helped her out of her mannish jacket in the stuffy darkness. Then they both stiffened, all over, when they heard that hall door open and somebody relit that wall fixture to shed wan light across the pressed tin and through the slit above. Had she dared to utter a sound, Portia might have allowed she followed his drift about a sly old boss.

Then they heard girlish giggles, and a voice Longarm had heard out yonder on that very chesterfield protested, "Ooh, we really shouldn't! I hope you don't think I'm that sort of a girl. But you have me so hot!''

Spooned in Longarm's lap with one shoulder against the black-painted glass and the other over the narrower gap between their windowsill perch and the backs of the filing cabinets, Portia bit her knuckles to keep from giggling herself as they both heard slurping, huffing, and puffing on the far side of the files. Longarm wriggled out of his own tweed coat and gun belt while they were at it, feeling sort of sweaty and left out as he detected the odor of a Havana perfecto in the still air of the unventilated hideout. It seemed some son of a bitch was enjoying a good smoke

12

and a French lesson at the same time out front!

Then the door popped open again and they heard the familiar voice of Billy Vail chortle, "Aha! I gotcha!"

Followed by: "Oops, sorry, ladies, I thought somebody else was in here! You ain't seen my deputy Custis Long, have you?"

Longarm wasn't surprised to hear Miss Bubbles from the stenograph pool coyly ask if they were talking about that tall, dark, and handsome one she'd seen in court. But he had to adjust his mental picture some when a less familiar female voice chimed in. "We just ducked in here for a little smoke and haven't seen a soul, Marshal Vail. You won't tell Judge Dickerson you caught us smoking, will you? He's such an old silly about women smoking or dipping snuff!"

Billy Vail's humor sounded somewhat restored as he gallantly replied, "Far be it from me to mention that fine cigar from His Honor's cigar box, Miss Wanda. I always say, if a man don't keep count of his own cigars, who else does he expect to count 'em?"

Then the couple hiding from the old gruff heard him laugh boyishly and shut the door after him as he left.

The tobacco thief called Wanda giggled and asked, "Do you think he'll tell on us?"

The aptly described buxom blonde, Miss Bubbles, calmly replied, "I doubt it. His Honor inspires more fear than loyalty with that holier-than-thou stone face he walks around behind. I wonder what that scamp Custis has been up to this time."

Wanda said, "Let me have a drag on that cigar, and then I suspect we ought to get back in the pool. Isn't Custis Long the one you said had a disappointing peanut to go with such a tall drink of water?"

Portia had to bite down hard, and Longarm felt his ears burning, when Miss Bubbles replied, "That was poor Hiram, the court recorder. There's nothing wrong with that old organ-grinder of Custis Long, as he likes me to call it.

13

I feared I'd weep the first time he showed that monster hard for me! But you're right, we'd better get rid of this cigar and back to the salt mines whilst we're still able!''

They left the wall fixture lit as they headed off along the hallway. So Longarm could see Portia's cold expression in the wan glow from above as she tried to twist off his lap and just made him harder while she hissed, ''You disgusting animal! At least that mining mogul's widow up on Capitol Hill has some class to her ass! Who was that revolting little slut you showed it to so hard for?''

Longarm sheepishly but honestly replied, ''Aw, Miss Bubbles ain't all that revolting, Miss Portia. Not being a man, you'll just have to take my word that few men would be able to show their old organ-grinders to Miss Bubbles *soft*!''

''You should be ashamed of yourself!'' she insisted. ''I should be ashamed of myself for ever having felt the least bit curious about that aptly described organ-grinder! That's all any of us mean to you and that instrument of torture you're so proud of, right?''

He shrugged, absently wondering what time it was getting to be, and calmly replied, ''I didn't know the enjoyment was so one-sided. From the way some ladies I've known wiggled and jiggled, I'd have sworn they were using and abusing me and my old grinder as much as I was— have it your own way—using and abusing *them* and their old ring-dang-doos. What are we arguing about, Miss Portia? You told me that night you threw me out that you never wanted to see me or my old organ-grinder again, and this awkward secret meeting was never *my* grand notion! I just want to get us out of this fix you got us into with all this nonsense about some old bawd's dirty diary.''

He gingerly lifted her by the hips to slide his own pelvis from under her weight so he could drop one leg into the slot between the marble sill and the backs of the file drawers, adding, ''I reckon it's as safe now as it's likely to get, if only I'm as double-jointed worming backwards! Hang on

14

to my hat, coat, and six-gun till I send for 'em, will you?''

Portia watched in wonder with the load in her lap as she was able to make out better what he'd done getting them in there in the first place. He'd confounded the liver and lights out of her in total darkness.

Longarm began by lowering himself to his knees on the long narrow strip of flooring behind the files. Then he contorted to push the back of a file drawer with a boot heel until it slid out the other way far enough for him to get first his boots and then his rump and then the rest of him through the tunnel left once he'd crawfished the drawer all the way out on the floor in front of the stacked files. Once on his feet again, on that side of the wall of file drawers, he shoved the drawer he'd displaced back where it belonged. Then he hauled another drawer all the way out and placed it atop the card table, before he bent to peer through at the level of that hidden windowsill and call out, "Shove all the loose stuff through and let me set it aside before I haul you out head first, hear?''

Then the door behind him opened again and Longarm muttered, "Shit!" as he realized too late he should have locked it when he had the chance.

But to his weak relief the junoesque blond stenographer known to one and all around the Denver Federal Building as Miss Bubbles asked, "What are you up to this morning, Custis? Your boss, Marshal Vail, was just asking about you!''

Longarm replied, "I noticed. Shut and bar that door for us, will you, Miss Bubbles? I'll explain all this as soon as I help another pal out through this rabbit hole.''

So Miss Bubbles did as she was told, and watched in blue-eyed wonder as Longarm hauled first his own stuff, then a handsome jacket and a marvelous hat from a rabbit hole indeed, followed by a fashionable but somewhat disheveled older woman Miss Bubbles had seen around the courtrooms on more formal occasions.

The two women eyed one another uncertainly as Long-

15

arm introduced each to the other as an old pal while he and Portia put themselves back together. He had to hope Miss Bubbles was on their side.

He said, "Miss Bubbles, I got to tear down the hall and mend some fences pronto. Would you show Miss Portia out that basement side exit and hide her out for me until lunchtime at that boardinghouse we both know across the way?"

Miss Bubbles hesitated, then grinned like the good sport and mean little kid everyone knew and loved, as often as possible, to tell the less certain lady lawyer, "Stick with me and I'll teach you lots of bad habits. I only came back here for the perfumed wax matches I'd left. I just love those decadent Mexican matches and jasmine-scented candles, don't you?"

Portia protested, "Custis, we have to talk!"

But Longarm was already on his way out the door and down the hall on the double. As he slid to a stop in the reception room of his home office, he found Marshal Vail out front, jawing with Henry. So Longarm said, "Howdy, gents. Heard you were looking for me. I've just been questioning a possible witness in connection with that Mulligan case."

To which the beetle-browed Billy Vail replied with a puzzled scowl, "How come? What do you know about the Mulligan case? We just got it handed to us this very morning, before you ever darkened that damned door! Have you suddenly added the gift of second sight to your other dubious achievements?"

When Longarm didn't answer, seeing as he had nothing to say, Billy Vail grumped, "Never mind all that. What have you found out so far about the Mulligan case?"

Chapter 3

Longarm tried, "Like I told that older woman in widow's weeds, I don't see any connection betwixt the case you just got this morning and that Madame Velvet dying over in Mulligan last week."

Vail beckoned to follow as he turned away, growling, "I read about that in the *Rocky Mountain News.* I remember when the madams Ruth Jacobs and Emma Gould were younger-looking too. What in thunder could the death of an aging courtesan by natural causes have to do with that post office robbery over in Mulligan, for Pete's sake?"

As he followed the older man into an oak-paneled and smoke-filled private office, Longarm replied in an easier tone, "That's what I told that courtesan or whatever just now, Boss. I told her I'd read about Madame Velvet on that obituary page, but saw nothing suspicious about a heart stroke, and knew even less about that robbery in town. Like you said, we just this morning learned about it!"

Vail waved at the one visitor's chair and circled his big cluttered desk to sink into his swivel chair as he snapped, "For which the Postmaster General will have my undying gratitude and I hope he chokes on it, the son of a bitch!"

Plucking an unlit stogie with a disgusting wet end from the ashtray atop a pile of telegrams, Vail added, "Have you ever noticed how those high-paid postal inspectors sit down to pee and call us in when they don't know their asses from their elbows?''

Then, to Longarm's horror, he stuck the sticky end of the stogie in his mouth and struck a match to light the stinkier end. So Longarm fished out one of his own three-for-a-nickel cheroots in self-defense as he marveled, as ever, at the prices some men were willing to pay for really rancid tobacco. He knew old Billy paid more than a nickel apiece for that make of cigar. It still looked like he was puffing on a dog turd, and it smelled even worse.

As Longarm found no ashtray provided for the leather-covered horsehair chair he was smoking in, he shook out the match and dropped it on the rug as usual. Billy Vail pretended not to notice as he exhaled a smoke cloud that would have made an octopus proud and explained to his senior deputy, ''You'll find the trail cold as a banker's heart, as we usually do by the time the tea-sipping Postmaster General calls us in to find the ball his fair-haired lads have dropped. But what can I tell you, old son? If you weren't a fair hand at cutting cold trails, you'd be riding for some less demanding outfit, such as the purple-pissing post office. So you won't need typed-up travel orders to put a livery nag on your regular expense account and drift on over to Mulligan, just down the Front Range from the Jefferson County seat at Golden. You'd best check in at the Drover's Rest and wire us as soon as you interview the local postmaster and find out what those postal inspectors missed.''

Longarm took a thoughtful drag on his cheroot, flicked some ash on the rug to discourage carpet mites, and started to ask a dumb question. But Billy Vail had already told him someone had robbed the post office in yonder little mining town, and since he'd just been ordered to ask them all about it at said post office, he felt no call to ask his boss any questions that were only likely to get him yelled at. Old Billy could be a caution when you asked him questions he had no answers for. So Longarm rose to his considerable height and said, "I'll borrow me a real pony from my pals at the Diamond K on the outskirts of town. I hate to chase outlaws on livery nags, and you did want me to see if I could cut their trail, right?"

Vail nodded grudgingly and replied, "That's about the size of it. I doubt any of the robbers will be anywhere within chasing distance by this time, though. According to the impossible report turned in by the postal inspectors who got there first to fuck things up, the gang of four came in on foot just before closing time, held everyone inside at gunpoint until the sun was setting, them scampered off into the tricky light of the mountain gloaming to vanish into thin air. The glorified office boys who asked the wrong folks the wrong questions were undecided as to whether four grown men with guns and bags of Uncle Sam's money dove down that rabbit hole to Wonderland after Miss Alice, or climbed up that rope to nowhere with the help of a visiting Hindu fakir. I want you to start from where they'd left their damned horses when they set out on foot to rob the one post office in one tiny little mining town, and don't say they ducked down in the one modest mine. Both the postal inspectors and mining company police agree on that much."

Longarm quietly asked if Vail would like to have him sit in his lap while he searched for leads in a town a good twenty miles or more away. Vail chuckled sheepishly and confessed, "It was a heap more fun when I got to go out in the field after the sons of bitches on my own. I can see why you keep fucking up, old son. At the rate you're going, they'll never promote you to a desk job."

Longarm allowed he sure hoped so, and left before Vail could ask him who that mystery woman he'd been talking to down the hall might have been. He waved an adios to Henry on the way out of the office, and got the hell out of the building in hopes of catching up with old Portia and Miss Bubbles before they could compare too many notes.

As he circled a beer dray to cross the busy street south of the Federal Building, he was hailed by the familiar trim figure in black that was Portia and Portia alone. As Longarm joined her in front of the brownstone rooming house he'd aimed both gals at, Portia told him, "I owe you an apology. I admit it. But how was I to know what a gallant fool you were when that poor lesbian bragged about the size of your virile member? You have to allow she described it much as I remember it from that night I thought I'd been invited to supper at a respectable restaurant. How could the poor thing have known enough to brag so convincingly to that other girl and, if the truth be known, to me?"

Longarm replied, "Lucky guess, I reckon," as he tried to figure out what in blue blazes she was talking about.

He tossed in, "I just got a good excuse to talk to you some more about your Madame Velvet. Seems somebody robbed the post office over in that same dinky mining town, and they'll be expecting me to canvass the whores and gamblers around town, along with anyone who knows any whores and gamblers. Gents who ride the owlhoot trail tend to hole up in the shadier parts of any town. I reckon outlaws who invested more of their ill-gotten gains on worthwhile goods and services or respectable real estate wouldn't have to ride the owlhoot trail. Rumor has it Frank and Jess have been living respectably and steering clear of the primrose path since they had such a close call at Northfield back in '76. But let's hope the outlaws who just struck over in Mulligan are still in the game for the fun of it."

Then he cautiously asked, "When did you first suspect Miss Bubbles was one of the lizzy gals, Miss Portia?"

The lady lawyer pointed with her chin and said, "Walk me up to the hack stand while I still have some shreds of my own reputation to cling to. You might have warned me about the poor thing. You might have told her I was not one of her kind, for heaven's sake. We'd no sooner got up to that room you asked her to take me to when she tried to kiss me and actually put a hand on my titty! I was so surprised I cursed out loud and demanded some explanations then and there!''

Longarm took her elbow to guide her around some dog shit on the walk as he soberly replied, ''I don't blame you. She sure don't strike most folks around the Federal Building as a lizzy gal. I hope she explained things to your satisfaction?''

Portia said, ''She did indeed. I felt so sorry for her, despite my distaste for her queer ways, as she burst into tears and told me how she feared for her government job and how sweet you'd been about not giving her away when she'd told them in desperation that she was your girl.''

Longarm managed not to laugh—it wasn't easy—as he modestly told Portia, ''It was the least I could do. She takes dictation just fine. But she's likely right that they'd fire any stenograph gal who acted queer around the others. I figured that had to be the reason she was telling that Miss Wanda I had a bigger dick than that court recorder. Miss Wanda likely thought Miss Bubbles had some way of knowing. Should we talk some more about Madame Velvet over at your place this evening, or did you have some other place in mind?''

Portia waved to a hack driver watering his draft horse at a curbside trough as she told Longarm, ''I don't know if I'm ready to have you darkening my own door in Denver again. But when I'm over yonder in Mulligan, I stay at the Drover's Rest when I'm not at Madame Velvet's place with her nieces. Needless to say, the address is no longer what you could truthfully call a house of ill repute. The one thing both spinsters agree upon is that neither cares to own and operate a whorehouse.''

Longarm allowed that in that case they'd likely meet up again over in the Front Range country, seeing they both had other business there. She said, and he agreed, it might be best if the heirs of Madame Velvet held off on trying to sell that nineteen-volume diary before he'd had time to take a gander at it and advise them on just how much fire they could be playing with.

Then he helped her up into the hack, and turned to head back to that rooming house as he consulted his pocket watch. It was still a tad early to leave any business office for noon dinner. But it was safe to say Miss Bubbles wouldn't have been sneaking off down the hall to begin with if she'd had many shorthand chores to tend to, and wherever she was, she sure had him confused. So he made sure Portia's hack was long gone, then ducked up into the boardinghouse he and Miss Bubbles both knew fairly well. Nobody popped out of the manager's door on the first floor as he passed. Folks who managed such places knew regulars would settle up later, but might not come by as regular if you made them uncomfortable.

At the head of the stairs Longarm turned to a door he remembered fondly, knocked, and went on in when a familiar voice called back in a mighty inviting manner.

He found Miss Bubbles under the covers of the one big bed in the middle of the room. The shades were drawn against the noonday sun, and the junoesque blonde's summer frock was neatly folded over the brass foot rails. So Longarm shut and barred the door, to hang his hat by it and start shucking the rest as he thoughtfully circled the foot of the bed, saying, "Let me guess. You told her I was helping you cover some wicked habits so you could cover some of *my* wicked habits?"

Miss Bubbles demurely replied, "I admired her hat, but she struck me as one of those jealous gals who expect to hog a natural man all to themselves. I could have told her no one-woman man would ever be enough of a man for *this* woman. But I thought it might be best for the three of us if I let her think she didn't have to worry about me. It may be harder for a man to understand, but a woman starting to go gray is inclined to worry about younger women with bigger tits. So I told her I admired her tits and wanted to suck on them. I knew that was a good way to get her mind off my feminine charms. I've learned from experience that there's nothing like another gal getting fresh to make some spoilsports dismiss her as a gal. I told her you were awfully sweet and that if ever I decided to try it with a man I might try it with you. I had no call to tell her it's only fun with poor pussy-licking Wanda when there's nobody else available.''

As Longarm hung his gun belt over the bedpost and sat down beside her to shuck his boots, Miss Bubbles chuckled and said, "She told me I had no idea what I've been missing. She said she was sorry she couldn't help me out, but that I'd been right about the size of your old organ-grinder. How would she know about the size of your old organ-grinder, Custis?''

Longarm soberly said, "Lucky guess?'' as he got rid of the last of his duds and tossed the covers aside to marvel, as ever, at the way a buxom blonde could seem put together under her peaches-and-cream skin as a collection of almost perfect spheres, neither too soft nor too firm, but just right, anywhere you squeezed her. Then he took her in his muscular bare arms and let her guide his raging erection into place between her pneumatic thighs.

As he entered her, Miss Bubbles gushed, "Ooh, yesss! Every time you put that in me it seems I'd somehow forgotten how swell it feels! Do you find my ring-dang-doo a pleasant surprise too, darling?''

He knew what she meant. But Miss Bubbles was not a philosophical sort of gal. She was just a good old gal and, as events had just proven, a real pal. So he told her truthfully, "It's always a swell surprise whether it's with something old, something new, something borrowed, or something blue.''

"You mean you want to screw me blue someplace down and dirty like way up my ass or deep down my throat?'' she asked uncertainly.

He laughed, thrust harder, and said, "We've only the lunch hour and it feels just fine, Miss Bubbles. I think one of the nicest surprises about you is that you're one of the few gals I know who takes an honest screwing for what it's meant to be, an interlude of pure and simple pleasure.''

She wrapped her legs around his waist and moved up and down in time with his thrusts as she calmly replied, "It feels sort of honest and, I don't know, *clean,* I reckon, to just fuck a pal for the pleasure with no shit about it never having been this way before. Do I fuck as nice as that flat-chested Portia who thinks it's wicked for anyone else in the world to fuck you?''

Longarm nuzzled her collarbone as he felt himself almost there and moaned, "Honey, right now, nobody in this whole wide world could ever fuck as nice as you!''

She dug her nails into his buttocks as she clamped down with her vaginal muscles and moaned, "I'm so glad. It feels so fine to know that right this moment we're the only lovers in the whole wide world who've ever come this way!''

Then she went limp in his arms and added, "Oh, that was lovely, and I hope I've left things so's you can still come as lovely with that skinny brunette, the poor jealous thing.''

Chapter 4

The mining town of Mulligan was starting to die on the vine, and it was closer to Denver on the map than by way of public transportation. Mulligan nestled in a north-south fold of the Front Range, and its one operational mine shipped ore by freight wagon to the smelters up in Golden. Most other goods and services moved in or out along that same dusty wagon trace, at right angles to the one pony trail running up into that stretch of the Front Range from Denver. So seeing he'd need some means of getting around once he got there, Longarm loaded his army McClellan, saddlebags, and Winchester '73 on one pony he'd borrowed off the Diamond K, loaded lighter trail supplies on a second, and headed on out that afternoon, hoping to make it before sundown.

The nights and some of the days were still nippy in the Rockies at that time of the year. So he took along a sheepskin coat as well as a stirrup-length rain slicker made of canary-yellow oilcloth by an outfit catering to both fishermen and cowboys, since they both had more trouble with Dame Nature than some thought. Most cows on the north ranges were roped with merchant-marine lines of hard-twist Kentucky hemp, and a summer storm west of Longitude 100° drove horizontal sheets of rain as hard as any nor'easter off the rock-ribbed coasts of old New England.

He wore that blamed tweed suit, seeing it was so close to Denver and the weather still cool enough, most of the time. But he balled up the shoestring tie and tucked it in a shirt pocket in the unlikely event President Rutherford Hayes and First Lady Lemonade Lucy showed up on an election-year tour of the Rockies. There was no need for chaps in the foothills of the Front Range, and Longarm ignored the constant advice to wear spurs on his low-heeled cavalry stovepipes. He did so for the same reasons that he preferred tracking men in low heels. It wasn't that much tougher to control your mount without spurs if you had any notion how to ride. But it could get awkward trying to sneak around in spurred high-heeled Justins, and even when you were simply walking around afoot in country or town, your feet held up longer on low heels.

He wasn't expecting to need either the Winchester or the extra trail supplies he'd brought along. But he'd learned the hard way that when a lawman found himself short of grub or firepower on the trail, it could be a bigger bother than just hauling the shit along to begin with.

As in the case of the fisherman's slicker, Longarm's saddle gun had been chosen for purely practical reasons. There were repeating carbines chambered for longer range or heavier stopping power. But the lever-action '73, chambered for the same .44-40 rounds as his six-gun, was good enough for Buffalo Bill and many another High Plains rider who just hated to fumble for two calibers of ammunition in the middle of a tense situation. With its carbine length, Longarm had thirteen rounds to work with if he carried one in the chamber, and all thirteen could stop a man sure at two hundred yards, or even four hundred with a lot of luck and elevation.

A lawman riding west from Denver into the Rockies had to consider such ranges. From the streets of the Mile High City of Denver, you could easily see the higher peaks of the Front Range. So eastern dudes were forever drifting west along Seventeenth Street for an after-dinner stroll to such nearby wonders. Denver folks with mean streaks just let 'em stroll. More kindly locals gently pointed out that the nearest lower slopes of the Front Range were fifteen or more miles away. You couldn't see *them* from Denver, of course. Those peaks that seemed to loom right outside of town were much farther away. The thin dry air at Denver's altitude made what should have seemed distant purple mountains look like nearby hills, complete with what seemed to be scattered trees and other sharply etched features. It was tough to sell strangers on the sheer size anything up yonder had to be to be visible from the streets of Denver.

As he rode out to the west that afternoon, up the far slopes of the South Platte flood plain to rolling prairie level with the so-called Capitol Hill on the far side of Downtown Denver, Longarm passed clay quarries, hog and produce farms, then bigger fields of sprouting grain, mostly barley for the breweries of the Mile High City. Any city drank a lot of beer. Beer didn't ship well, and barley grew better than a lot of other crops in Denver's patch of the High Plains. A few miles farther west, the prairie rose inconveniently for the plow, and was a bit dry for cows once the greenup had come to the mountain parks off to the near west. So he and his two borrowed ponies had a lot of foothill range to travel that still looked much the same as it had back in what Mister Lo, the poor Indian, called his Shining Times.

Neither Mister Lo nor the buffalo he'd used as his general store were to be seen that close to Denver anymore. So in point of fact the raw landscape all around was likely more as it had been before humankind of any breed had ridden nearby. Grazing buffalo, prairie elk, and pronghorn would have kept the spring greenup all around as neatly trimmed as the recently departed winter cattle. Longarm knew that by the Fourth of July the rolling swells all about would be covered with a tawny carpet of summer-cured short grass the color of a sleeping lion's hide, with here and there a clump of spinach-green soap weed, a northern variety of the better-known yucca of the Southwest. Hidden by the grass and greater forbs, an occasional small cactus pad waited like a mean little kid for some bare ass to squat over it. The chili-pepper-red bulldog ants the tourists and new kids in town found so interesting could sting worse than any cactus growing that far north.

There were no trees to be seen unless you knew where to look for trees in such country. As the swells rose ever higher, like waves rolling west against a higher shore, some began to crest like ocean breakers, with outcrops of brick red sandstone in place of foaming whitecaps. Such frozen-in-place breaking waves were called hogbacks because, from right angles, you could say the gentle eastard flanks looked something like processions of humpy hogs with raw spines lined up to charge north or south along the slopes of the higher Rockies to the west. The post road Longarm was following led through notches in such hogbacks, of course. If you looked sharp you'd see patches of lettuce-green crack willow and more silvery cottonwood, watered by the natural drainage between the higher windswept swells and outcrops. No trees grew close to the more traveled trail, not this close to any market for convenient firewood.

Longarm resisted many a temptation to scout an inviting side-draw as he stuck to the well-traveled pony track, noting how little the dust ahead had to tell him.

They'd had a wet spring after a long recent drought, but it hadn't rained worth mentioning since that post office robbery seventy-odd hours earlier. So *some* of the many hoofprints heading his way from the mining town up ahead *could* have been left by one or more of those outlaw riders. But he'd been over Henry's transcribed reports from the Postmaster General, and there'd been nothing about any suspects mounted on camels or even unusually shod horses.

28

And the outlaws could have headed north to Golden, south to Buffalo Creek, or west to Idaho Springs just as easily as along the most obvious escape route toward the Denver railroad yards. South along the Front Range, toward faraway Buffalo Creek, through wilder, less settled country, made the most sense for owlhoot riders who really craved privacy along the owlhoot trail. But Longarm knew many such riders fled high and wide to the nearest, biggest town they could make it to. And those reports assured Longarm that the Jefferson County posses had scouted every wagon trace and game trail out of Mulligan for such sign as four loping ponies might have left in recent memory, all to no avail. Nobody around Mulligan could say for certain the sons of bitches *hadn't* ridden off on camels, although Longarm felt it was as likely they'd split up after the robbery.

Such simple tactics had saved Frank and Jesse after that Northfield robbery went sour on their gang. The posse could only track down so many at a time. So the brothers James had gotten away clean while the law tracked down Charlie Pitts and the Younger brothers. And *that* time the posse riders had known what the outlaws they were tracking looked like! From the little passed on to the Justice Department from the Postmaster General's office, all Longarm could accept as probable was that four masked figures in ankle-length canvas dusters had come into the Mulligan post office late in the afternoon on foot, held one and all at gunpoint until the sun was setting, and left on foot with cash and cash alone from the office safe.

They'd avoided the usual mistakes with postal money orders, filled out or blank, and taken no stamps to use as small change along the way and be remembered as strangers in town by shopkeepers, bartenders, or hash slingers along their escape route. They'd taken the cash kept on hand to redeem or pay for postal money orders, and left with nothing at all likely to point back down such a trail or trails as they'd followed out of town. The Postmaster

General was being a real sport about letting other lawmen in on the action.

The mental map in his head told him he had just about another hour to ride. So Longarm resisted the temptation to light another smoke as he sang:

> Farther along, we'll know more about it.
> Farther along, we'll understand why.
> Cheer up, my brothers, walk in the sunshine,
> We'll understand it all by and by.

And half a mile up the trail, one of the two riders hunkered behind the red rimrock of a hogback sneered, "Listen to him, will you? He's singing a church song as if this was the Sabbath and he was on his way to a Sunday-Go-to-Meeting-on-the-Green! Didn't they tell us old Longarm was supposed to be a cut above tough?"

The younger of the two had the sights of a Sharps .50-170 zeroed on the next rise to their east, a point-blank range for a Big Fifty meant to drop buffalo at ten thousand yards if you knew what you were doing. Pecos Tim liked to think he knew what he was doing, so he said, "Never mind his damned singing and mind you back my single-shot with that repeating Spencer. For Longarm's said to be more than tough if you *miss* him. They say he moves like armed and dangerous spit on a hot stove!"

So the riders waiting for him kept their heads down as Longarm rode toward them, singing the one church song that still made sense to a man who'd lived through more than one sudden fork in his future by the time he'd lived long enough to vote and shave regularly.

The older killer levered a nervous round into the chamber of his Spencer, realized what he'd just done when the live round he'd loaded earlier gleamed accusingly up at him from the grass he lay in, and whispered, "Let him get closer. Don't fire until you see the whites of his eyes!"

The younger and hence less nervous of the pair snorted in a louder tone, "Shit, do you believe that tall tale about Bunker Hill, pard? Nobody with a lick of sense ever gave such an order to men armed with muzzle-loading flintlocks! By the time you can make out the whites of a man's eyes, he's too fucking *close* if you're pointing a *Gatling* gun his way."

He trained his Big Fifty through a cleft in the outcrop they were hiding behind as he added, "I'll take him when he tops that lower rise betwixt hither and yon. I make it around five hundred yards or hardly any elevation for old Pissfire here!"

"That's too far! What if you miss?" his more anxious partner bitched.

So the man with the Big Fifty sneered, "Run along home and hide under the bed if this chore is too big a boo for you. Me and old Pissfire never miss at five hundred yards, as I am about to show you!"

The one with the Spencer moaned, "Oh, Jesus!" as the two ponies and a good part of Longarm dropped from view behind the rise in the trail they'd been talking about. Then the bobbing head of the paint Longarm was riding rose back into view, along with Longarm from the midsection up. So the one aiming the buffalo gun his way pulled his set-trigger first to free the hair-trigger, as he squinted through the calibrated leaf sight to zero in on the crown of Longarm's Stetson, aiming to put seven hundred grains of lead through his heart, then with malice aforethought, let fly with his awesome weapon.

The space between them and their target filled with the billowing white cloud generated by 170 grains of black powder. As it cleared, they saw both Longarm's borrowed ponies tearing back the way they'd come, with that paint running wild under an empty saddle.

"You got him!" called the one with the Spencer in sick relief.

The one who'd fired the still-smoking Big Fifty chortled, "I was aiming to. I see his hat landed upside down in that

31

soap weed to the north of the trail. Cover me whilst I move in with my six-gun to have mercy on the cocksucker if he's still breathing.''

''Be careful!'' the one with the Spencer cautioned as the sharpshooter laid his empty buffalo rifle aside and rose to draw his Colt .36 Navy Conversion and step over the worn teeth of the outcrop. He was feeling good as he strode down the gentler slope to the east with the low afternoon sun warm on his back through his denim jacket. It made a man feel sort of like a god, or less like poor white trash at any rate, to down a man who'd never be able to question his grit again. It wasn't right to question the grit of a poor boy who'd never had the chance to explain about that night when he'd run out ahead of his kin as their cabin caught fire. When you gunned a man at long range, he never got to look you in the eye with those unspoken questions hanging in the air like invisible haunts.

As he moved in closer, he told the dead lawman's hat over yonder how sick he'd been getting about all those yarns about its famous former owner. He taunted, ''Longarm this and Longarm that! Longarm did wonders and et cucumbers and never had to shit or pay for pussy like the rest of us, and didn't I ever clean his plow for him just now!''

Then as he topped that same rise from his own side of it, Longarm fired from his prone position in the dusty grass, and the man who'd just shot him out of his saddle, or thought he had, felt his unfired six-gun slipping from his tingling fingers as he stared up at all that gathering darkness to wistfully say to the little swarming stars before his dying eyes, ''Jesus H. Christ! I seem to be shot in the chest, and how could *that* have happened?''

Chapter 5

What had happened was that sound traveled around seven hundred miles an hour, black powder shoved a bullet five hundred miles an hour, and light moved way faster than either. So it was just possible to duck a well-aimed bullet at long range when you didn't waste time wondering what was happening.

Longarm had instinctively thrown himself and caution to the wind the moment he saw a flame-centered ball of cotton blossoming atop that hogback up ahead. The whip-crack report had snapped at his ears a fraction of a second before Death had plucked at one sleeve with as much lead as it took to down a buffalo. Then the grass had come up to knock some wind out of him, and he could only hope those damned horses wouldn't lope all the way home to the Diamond K with his Winchester and possibles.

There was nothing a man who'd been drygulched could do but get his six-gun out and train it on the skyline ahead as he lay low and just waited until, sure enough, there was an asshole standing yonder with another six-gun.

Longarm went on lying low once he'd dropped his own target in plain view and decided he didn't have to worry about anything spread out across the grass as still as that. Then a million years later, he heard the sweet sound of two

33

ponies, moving off to the west at a dead run. The backup rider had chickened out. The backup rider was usually less of a shooter than the cuss who'd brought him along.

First things coming first, Longarm rose on one elbow to gaze back the way he'd been coming from. The spooked ponies had bolted around three furlongs before they'd managed to foul the long lead line running from the swells of Longarm's McClellan to the bridle of the chestnut pack pony. So they were both grazing the still-green buffalo grass just off the trail as they waited for somebody to untangle some damned rope from a soap-weed clump.

Longarm figured it was better to risk being stranded on foot than shot in the back. So he rose to move up the rise in a crouch and drop to his belly and elbows behind the sprawled body of the one he knew he didn't have to worry about anymore.

As he kept one eye on those weathered red rocks that rifle shot had come from, Longarm searched the still-warm victim of his own marksmanship. In life the cuss had tried hard to look like an average cowhand of, say, thirty, in need of a shave and a haircut but not to any distinguishing extent. In addition to two ammo belts, one for his revolver and the other for that Big Fifty, the cuss had died with an old wallet boasting over a hundred dollars in new silver certificates.

Longarm pocketed the thirty-eight dollars in hard cash as well, but hung on to the wallet in the unlikely event someone from the Denver Public Library would recall issuing the new library card to one Paul Jones, who seemed to live at the same address as Madame Emma Gould. It was possible some of Madame Emma's soiled doves might recall the bushy brows and scarred upper lip. Men who recalled the street numbers of whorehouses were inclined to have visited them more than once.

Leaving the dead man where he lay, just a short ways out of town, Longarm gathered his grit, leaped to his feet, and zigzagged up to flop down some more behind the red sandstone spine of the hogback. When nothing happened, he risked a bareheaded peek over the rimrocks to see he had the whole crest all to himself. He rose and moved down the far side to pick up and pocket a red-and-white-striped paper bag.

Then he legged it back the other way, picked up and put on his hat, and told the man he'd shot not to go away while he moved slowly back along the trail toward those grazing ponies.

You never knew about critters. Sometimes a pony or a jackrabbit seemed to want to play, the way those big gray grasshoppers with butterfly wings liked to play with you, pretending they didn't notice your approach until they buzzed just out of reach again, as if they were laughing at you.

But while the paint wearing his saddle and Winchester walleyed him some, neither pony was up to fighting good Kentucky hemp wrapped three times around the root-crowns of solidly set soap weed. So he soon had both horses under control, and while he was at it, changed saddles to ride the steadier chestnut and let the high-strung paint tote the packsaddle behind him.

None of this took all that long. So he was soon on his way and in less than an hour, as he'd promised earlier, he topped the last hogback east of town to ride down its steeper west slope into the shoestring settlement of Mulligan, Colorado. It was named for a prospector who'd sold out too soon, and resembled a shoestring with the way it was strung out along one main street and drainage ditch running north and south near the center of the long natural fold. The hoist and toolsheds of the Mulligan silver mine formed another more compact clump about two hundred yards up the far slope. One-family shacks of unpainted frame with tarpaper roofs were spread helter-skelter anywhere they'd landed, as if some giant child had tossed shabby building blocks across the raw earth. Mine tips, trash dumps, and what looked like an acre of grave markers were upslope from the drainage ditch and built-up business street. There were no trees and damned little grass to be seen within sight of the dinky town. As Longarm rode down into it with the sunset staring him in the face, the ruddy glow outlined the black silhouettes of others, mounted or afoot, who seemed to find him a thundering wonder to behold as they came up the bare slope to hail him and demand he state his name and business.

Longarm reined in and called back, "I ain't here to rob your post office at sundown, gents. They sent me to look into that for you. I'd be the law. Federal. U.S. Deputy Marshal Custis Long of the Denver District Court, and I just now shot an unfortunate who might have had something to do with that robbery. So I need a little help with that before we get into anything else around here!"

A man in the lead, who'd drawn close enough for Longarm to make out a silvery star, matching hair, and a low-slung Schofield .45, called back, "I'd be Undersheriff Warren Babcock and we've been expecting you, Longarm. You say you just shot somebody?"

Longarm dismounted to seem less imperious and make a tougher target as he replied, "About three miles out. Answering to the name of Paul Jones, which seemes unlikely, and packed a Navy Colt and a Big Fifty along with a scarred upper lip. I sure hope he wasn't some popular local figure."

The locals chewed on that between them, and when none of the mumbles seemed to be taking them anywhere, Undersheriff Babcock decided, "Not anybody famous in these parts, Longarm. Wasn't the real Paul Jones a navy man?"

Longarm nodded, but said, "Colt named his lighter six-guns after the navy to distinguish them from his heavier army dragoons. You didn't have to be in either service to buy one new, and what'll you bet the one I have now in a saddlebag passed through many a pawnshop since they made it in Hartford back around '61 as a cap-and-ball? A pal he rode with seems to have carried off his Big Fifty. I know it was a Big Fifty because I recognized the ammunition he was packing for it, and I'm glad as all get-out he *missed*!''

Undersheriff Babcock said he'd send a buckboard out for the son of a bitch before the night critters could get to him. Meanwhile, the older lawman assured Longarm that they'd be proud to put him up at the Babcock house if he liked grits and gravy and didn't mind kids.

As they all started back down the slope with Longarm leading the Diamond K stock, Longarm said, ''That's right neighborly of you, but Marshal Vail's expecting to contact me at your Drover's Rest, and speaking of which, I didn't notice any telegraph poles along my way out from Denver.''

Babcock said, ''I'll tell the wife to leave the best china be then. That pony track you were following is the shortest mail route east, which is likely why them post office riders pointed it out to you. But we ship out ore to Golden up the way, and freight in supplies from there, and Western Union's wires follow that route as well. You say another one got away from you with a buffalo rifle three miles or so out of Mulligan?''

Longarm replied, ''Yep. If it's any comfort, I'd say he was packing a yellow streak as well as a Sharps .50-170. He'd have had this child pinned down tight with that longer-range weapon if he'd stood his higher ground. He might or might not have hung on to the Big Fifty. If he's smart as well as yellow, he'll have gotten rid of it by now. I have no idea what he, she, or it looks like without it.''

Another man in the group volunteered, ''Nobody of any description rid through Mulligan today with a Sharps of such distinction. Come to study on it, I don't recall any strangers at all, riding in or out, save for that Denver gal who come down by coach from Golden an hour or so ago.''

Another townie said, ''That warn't no stranger. You're talking about that lady lawyer working for them Gilliam sisters. The ones Madame Velvet left her whorehouse to.

This lawman's looking for *strangers* of the *male* persuasion. What would he ever do with that lady lawyer?''

Longarm had been thinking about that all the way out from Denver as he recovered from the beating from Miss Bubbles. But he kept the thoughts to himself, seeing Portia had said she'd be staying at the one hotel in town.

As they all crossed the nearly dried-out drainage ditch, watching where they planted their heels on the smelly damp sand, Longarm produced that colorful paper bag he'd recovered near the site of that ambush and asked Undersheriff Babcock if it meant anything.

Babcock said, ''Sure. It's from Levine's Creamery and Candy Store, up near the schoolhouse. Nobody else in town sells chocolate drops, jawbreakers, and such in them candy-cane bags. They'd be closed by now, though. Riders coming into town after sundown ain't inclined to suffer sweet teeth. Why are we talking about candy stores, Deputy Long?''

Longarm said, ''Found this empty bag out where they were laying for me by the trail. It's possible some other traveler tossed it aside. A heap of reformed drunks chew hard candy to keep their cravings under control. This druggist gal I used to know told me alcohol and sugar are chemical kissing cousins. And a heap of owlhoot riders seem to have drinking problems. Drinking problems tend to drive some men off along the owlhoot trail. Bag smells as if there was licorice in it sometime today.''

The older lawman replied, ''So what? Lots of folk like licorice and as you just said yourself, anybody could have tossed that paper bag away once they et all the licorice.''

''Do you like licorice, pard?'' asked Longarm quietly.

Babcock hesitated, then grudgingly admitted, ''Well, mebbe not *personal*. But my older boy chaws a licorice whip every chance he gets. Is that supposed to mean something?''

Longarm said, ''Yep. How do you feel about the color yellow? Could you abide a room with canary-yellow walls?''

Babcock seemed on surer footing as he nodded and said, "Sure I could. My old woman allowed the shade was *buttercup* and never mentioned canary when she was picking out the paint. But our kitchen is still yellow with white trim, and just what are you accusing me and mine of, Deputy Long?"

Longarm said, "Nothing. My boss, Marshal Vail, called what I just done the process of elimination when he taught it to us early on. I should hardly need to tell a senior lawman that you often have more suspects than you can shake a stick at. It helps a heap if you can whittle your list down by eliminating the less likely ones."

Putting the candy-store bag away again he continued. "I can't tell you why, but licorice as a flavor and yellow as a color hit a heap of folks harder than most others. Some folks just can't get enough licorice, whilst others can't stand the taste. The color yellow seems to hit the human eye as strong. Most folks find yellow a cheerful tone. Those who don't care a lot for yellow tend to say it's their least favorite color and then some. So this housepainter I know tells me hotels and other such places catering to heaps of strangers passing through are well advised to avoid yellow walls, bedspreads, and such. Most of us seem to be able to take red and blue or leave them alone. But when we don't like yellow, or licorice candy, look out!"

The undersheriff grudgingly conceded, "I'm commencing to follow your drift. You aim to ask at Levine's Creamery about strange riders with Big Fifty buffalo guns and a craving for licorice, right?"

Longarm said, "That's about the size of it, after I canvass some of the more important possible witnesses. Our Mr. Paul Jones was sort of sneaky with library cards. He might have been sneaky about buying unusual ammunition for a buffalo gun they've ceased production on. So I find it sometimes pays to look into other purchases suspects might have made. Caught a train robber up Wyoming way one time because he would send out at night for Chinese grub and your average Wyoming rider has never even heard of it. Eliminating a whole lot of other Wyoming riders in and about Cheyenne, I only had to follow a Chinese delivery boy and . . . I better see about livery stalls for these ponies before I go over to the Drover's Rest I see yonder.''

That transaction took but a moment. Longarm didn't insult the old hostler in charge at the livery by telling him to make sure he watered the ponies before he foddered them. He left his harness and trail gear in the tack room, but took his saddle and Winchester '73 across to the Drover's Rest and hired himself a room for later.

As he was signing in, he failed to see Portia Parkhurst's name in the register, and there was an entry near the top of the page dated two days earlier. Feeling no call to ask questions about an unmarried lady in the smoke-filled lobby of a dingy small-town hotel, Longarm turned to Undersheriff Babcock and declared, ''Once I store this gear upstairs I mean to wire my home office about that shoot-out and grab me a late supper before I set out to canvass witnesses to that post office robbery. Where will your buckboard crew be bringing that dead body this evening?''

Babcock replied, ''Doc Maytag's cellar, under his drugstore. Doc's our deputy coroner when he ain't filling prescriptions. You won't find nobody at the post office at this hour. They close at six. Everybody will have gone home to supper hours ago.''

Longarm demanded, ''Where do they generally *eat* supper, in Paris, France? I got most of the home addresses in my notebook here. So like I said, Western Union, the nearest chili parlor, and some friendly evening house calls before I call it a day.''

Babcock shrugged and said, ''You can try. That ain't saying old Ash Woodside, our postmaster, is likely to take it friendly.''

To which Longarm calmly replied, ''Tough shit. They sent me out your way to look into your post office robbery, not to win any popularity contests.''

Chapter 6

The older undersheriff ran home while Longarm supped on corned beef and cabbage next to the stage depot, but Babcock must not have been too interested in his wife's best china or yellow kitchen walls. He caught up with Longarm later in time to order his own serviceberry pie with cheddar cheese and black coffee. He seemed to think a lawman he'd read about in both the *Denver Post* and *Rocky Mountain News* knew something new about cutting a trail that was seventy-two hours old and likely messed up by earlier lawmen putting words in the mouths of witnesses.

Babcock was surprised when Longarm stopped first at the cottage of a little old widow woman who'd only been in the post office near closing time when those strangers came in to rob it. She admitted she'd never worked there, and only dropped by once a month to pick up her widow's pension. When Longarm asked how she knew the four figures wearing feed-sack masks and floor-length travel dusters had been strangers, she stammered that they'd simply *seemed* like strangers as they waved those guns and talked so mean to everybody. When pressed, she had to allow there was no way to be certain all four of them were white men, or even men, when you considered everybody sounded much the same while whispering through burlap.

They went over Longarm's onionskin copy of her earlier interview with the postal inspectors and Undersheriff Babcock. Longarm didn't catch her changing anything important, but noted a few details she'd only left out because she'd never been asked, such as whether any of them had been wearing spurs or had she smelled licorice or Macassar oil.

When she allowed she'd been too scared to pay attention to such tomfoolery, Longarm thanked her, put his notes away, and led Babcock on up the slope to question a Cousin Jack who'd been posting a letter home to his kin in the mining country of Cornwall, England. Along the way the undersheriff asked how hair oil had entered into the case.

Longarm explained, "The rifleman I shot this afternoon had enough Macassar oil combed into his dark hair to grease a Baldwin locomotive. Like Big Fifty cartridges and licorice candy, you have to buy fancy hair oil along the way, see?"

Babcock replied, "I reckon. Are we looking for a suspect who eats licorice and combs Macassar oil into his curly locks whilst loading a Sharps .50-170 in a hideout with yellow walls?"

Longarm chuckled and said, "Not hardly. The one I shot used fancy hair oil for certain and likely bought his unusual ammunition. But either one of them could have liked licorice, and my remarks about some folks loathing yellow was only meant by way of illustration. I've no idea whether the one I got or the one who got away grew up hating or just loving any particular color. You have to go easy on this here eliminating, lest you scratch somebody off you list that really ought to be considered."

The interview with the mining man who spoke with a Cornish accent went smooth enough, Cousin Jacks speaking English plain enough unless they didn't want you to overhear them plotting against the boss, in which case they used their ancient and obscure Celtic lingo. The Cousin Jack recalled the robbery the same as the old widow woman

42

had, but was able to tell them the one holding a gun on him close up had been packing a Remington five-shooter .45. On the way out the same cuss had jingled, as if he might have been wearing Texican spurs. Neither cavalry nor tight-roweled North Range spurs were inclined to jingle. As the lawmen were leaving, Babcock allowed he was commencing to admire this process of eliminating. He declared, "We ain't just keeping an eye peeled for strangers in general. At least one of 'em packs that undersized version of the Colt .45, and a gent who favors Southwest spurs might be expected to crease his Texas hat like a greaser too!"

Longarm warned, "It's too early to draw that tight a mental picture of even one of 'em. You let your eyes hang open and worry about such details when you spy 'em. Outlaws have been known to brandish unusual details deliberately. I feel better about personal tastes in candy, hair oils, and such because a man's less likely to notice what he smells like, with or without a mask over his fool face."

They came next to the mustard siding and spinach trim of the more imposing Woodside house, set back behind pickets under a mansart roof shingled with real slate and trimmed with copper-gone-green.

Mr. Ashley J. Woodside, "Ash" to the many drinking pals of a small-town politician, was the portly white-haired elder of a far-flung postal clan, according to what Undersheriff Babcock had told Longarm on the way over. Ash Woodside had brothers running other small-town but full-time post offices under the reorganized Post-Reconstruction Hayes Administration in the old South as well as the new West. He had nephews and one son riding as postal inspectors, and didn't hesitate to tell Longarm, as they were being introduced on his front porch, that no Justice Department riders would have been invited in had it been up to *him*.

He didn't invite either lawman inside, or give them a good reason why, if he had any. So the three of them stood out there in the evening breezes while Longarm made him go over the whole tale of woe for what Woodside swore was the eighth or ninth damned time.

Longarm said soothingly, "Your boy and his cousins would have likely done it better, sir. For example, I noticed, reading over the reports of some lesser lights, that nobody thought to ask you how those four outlaws got you to open the safe for them."

Ash Woodside bristled, "I never did! Had the safe been locked when they made their move, I'd have gone to my grave like that heroic bank teller in Northfield before I'd have opened any damned safe filled with my uncle Sam's money for such trash!"

Longarm nodded soberly and insisted, "*Somebody* let 'em at over thirty thousand in cash. How many on the premises had the combination?"

Woodside blustered, "Nobody but myself! Two can keep a secret if one of them be dead. So I've left the combination in a sealed envelope in case anything happens to me. But not even my wife has ever read it since I reset it when I took over here. You see, you can reset the combination of a modern Mosler safe with these dials on the inside of the door and . . ."

"I know how you change the combination on a safe," Longarm declared. "You were fixing to tell me how four total strangers got the combination that evening."

The portly postmaster puffed, "They never did. The safe was open when they made their move. They must have been watching from outside. This young lady had just made out a postal money order to relatives in Saint Lou, and so I was just putting the money away for safekeeping when the place was suddenly filled with masked men with guns and I was rudely shoved on my behind with the safe wide open. There was no way I could stop them from just helping themselves. They did so, then and there. But then they held us all at gunpoint past our usual closing time, and to tell the truth I was afraid they meant to kill us, until at long last, once of them hissed like a snake and the four of them lit out in the gathering dusk. They'd allowed us no lamps inside as the sun went down. I suppose people passing on the street must have thought we'd already closed for the evening. One of the gunmen slammed the door shut on us after setting the night latch. But of course I had my key, once we got over the first confusion. As I've told everyone else more than once, by the time I could get out on the street to hue and cry, they were nowhere to be seen. A piano had started up in the saloon across the way, and I had to yell like hell before Warren here showed up.''

Warren Babcock agreed. ''Old Ash sure acted mad as a wet hen, and who could blame him? For the robbing sons of bitches had got away as slick as whistles. I naturally formed a posse comitatus and put it out on the telegraph wires. We never cut any trail worth shit once the sun came up again. The four of them appeared out of nowheres and disappeared back the way they came!''

''Five,'' said Longarm. ''There were five of them at least, counting the feminine finger coming in to send a money order just at closing time.''

The postmaster and the local law exchanged stricken looks in the dim lamplight making it outside through lace curtains. Undersheriff Babcock sheepishly murmured, ''Oh, shit, I never thought to follow up on that stranger gal, Ash! I remember asking you who she was, and when you said you hadn't known her, I let it go like the big-ass fool this federal man must take me for!''

Longarm gently suggested, ''You may not have investigated as many armed robberies as me, no offense. I ain't all that sharp. It said in your own report a customer unknown to Ash here came in just before the robbery to send a money order. I figure there must be, what, five or six hundred residents of a town this size, with fewer than that having occasion to use the post office much. So what did this total stranger sending money home at twilight *look* like, Mr. Woodside?''

The no-longer-puffed-up postmaster sheepishly admitted,

"You know, I can't really say! She was a mousy little thing, dressed in fusty-brown or maybe spiderweb-gray winter duds. I do recall feeling sorry for her not having a spring hat to call her own and, let's see, as I recall she wanted to send a fifty-dollar money order to her kin back in Saint Lou. *They* got her fifty dollars, of course. For I'd given her the money order and if she sent it, the post office in Saint Lou will be honor-bound to cash it."

Longarm nodded and said, "We'd best follow up on that then. I'll need to copy the names and addresses she gave you for that money order, whether she made them up or not. You call it eliminating when you make sure a doxy fooling us with fake names and addresses was really a doxy fooling us with fake names and addresses. Sometimes ladies *do* come into a post office near closing time just to send a money order to someone in Saint Lou."

Ash Woodside nodded gravely and said he'd get right to it in the morning, explaining his records of the mystery woman's transaction were locked in his desk down at the post office.

Longarm shook his head and said, "I don't want 'em in the morning. I want 'em *now*, Mr. Woodside."

The postmaster blinked and complained, "I'm in my slippers and we were fixing to turn in soon. Can't it wait till regular business hours?"

Longarm said, "They don't keep regular business hours along the owlhoot trail. It's rid by crooks at *all* hours, with the hours of darkness preferred and a rider in any hurry averaging nine miles an hour. So put on some damned shoes and let's get that new shit about money orders and such on the wire before anybody can ride another thirty miles or more! The dots and dashes of Mr. Morse move a hell of a lot faster than nine miles an hour. So with any luck we can have that mystery woman's money order confirmed or denied by the time you were fixing to open up in the morning. I have a pal on the Saint Lou police who'll be proud to join the milkman on his early morning rounds!"

So Ash Woodside went inside to put his shoes on and tell his wife she'd have to start without him at their usual bedtime if she wasn't willing to wait up a spell.

While he was inside, old Undersheriff Babcock beamed at Longarm and declared, "I've just eliminated something. Them stories about you in the *Denver Post* weren't bullshit after all!"

Longarm shrugged modestly and said, "Yes, they were. I'd warned that Reporter Crawford not to make me out as Denver's answer to Mr. Allan Pinkerton. But he will go on every time I get lucky tracking owlhoot riders."

The older but less experienced lawman shook his head and insisted, "You got more than *luck* going for you, old son! You know what you're doing, and I can see why those drygulchers were laying for you now! I wouldn't want a lawman of your caliber reading over *my* shoulder whilst I was planning devilment neither. So the mastermind those two were riding for wanted them to eliminate you before *you* could get to eliminating *them*! It's all so simple once you study on it!"

Longarm smiled thinly and replied, "No, it ain't. Seventy-two hours ago, and still counting, they pulled off a smooth professional robbery and got away clean. So why should they feel that hot-and-bothered by just one more lawman riding out this way to sniff a cold trail?"

He let that sink in. Then, as Ash Woodside was coming back out to rejoin them, Longarm added, "Unless their trail ain't all that cold, or long, or unless they're planning even more devilment in the very near future?"

The older lawman whistled softly and decided, "I reckon I can sort of eliminate you a possible answer. If they could be sure they were total strangers to a lawman with your rep, you wouldn't be making them so nervous! So what'll you bet at least someone in the bunch has to be a Colorado rider you already know?"

Then he added, "Know to be a crook, I mean!"

Longarm said, "No bet. I don't like them odds at all."

Chapter 7

One trouble with lighting up the one post office in a town long after its regular closing hours was that local folks kept pounding on the door and looking upset when you wouldn't let them in. So Undersheriff Babcock went out on the walk, hailed one of his deputies from across the way, and posted him at the door to explain they were investigating that recent robbery. More than one farmer or stockman from the surrounding hill country still wanted to save another ride into town by buying some damned stamps or posting a damned letter anyhow. To his credit, old Ash Woodside told that deputy to take their damned letters and set them on the sill till he could take care of them. Longarm decided he wasn't a mean old cuss. He was just used to bossing others about.

Woodside showed Longarm the ledger he recorded money-order transactions in. Money coming in to purchase postal money orders got entered in one column in black ink. Money paid out to customers cashing a money order from elsewhere was recorded in red ink in another column. Ash had neatly written the names of customers sending or receiving in the same red and black ink. Longarm noticed an Elvira Tenkiller in red above the black Mildred French who'd been sending that fifty-dollar money order when those masked men barged in.

When asked, the postmaster shook his head and said, "Miner's widow. Gets a monthly money order from the Indian Territory. Not a witness nor even a white woman. She left just before that more mysterious and mousy Mildred French came in, the sneaky sass! I never suspected her until you showed me the error of my ways. And to think I felt sorry for her and worried that a gal who couldn't afford a spring hat might be hard-pressed to spare that fifty dollars home!"

Local addresses had been listed under both names. Longarm wrote the both of them in his notebook as he decided, "I'd best scout the street number given by this Mildred French directly. I reckon the Cherokee widow can wait until a more reasonable hour to come calling."

Undersheriff Babcock smiled uncertainly and said, "I have been told Miss Elvira and her man, the late Gene Tenkiller, were Cherokee or, leastways, Cherokee breeds. All five of them eastern Civilized Tribes have intermarried with the neighbors to where hardly any of 'em is a pure anything. But how did you know that young widow was Cherokee in the first place?"

Longarm smiled thinly and said, "I could show off and pontificate about Cherokee and Cousin Jacks both being commonplace in Colorado mining country for the same reasons. But in point of fact Tenkiller is a common Cherokee name. Since they've took to holding property in the white man's way, with deeds and last wills and testaments to go with marriage licenses, birth certificates, and such, Cherokee have started to use family names, the same as us, for the same reasons. I know a heap of Cherokee Tallchiefs who ain't chiefs or all that tall. But once you get used to that, our way works better for keeping family records."

He put his notebook away as he added, "It's a long shot. But if a mere man noticed that that mysterious Mildred wasn't dressed right for a greenup, another *woman* of any

49

complexion might have paid more attention. So come morning, I mean to ask the Widow Tenkiller if she passed any mousy white stranger in town on that walk out front."

Old Babcock told old Woodside, "He calls that eliminating." Then he asked Longarm, "What was that about Cherokee mining men? I know you see Cherokee but hardly any other Indians working out our way as mining men. I've always found that curious. But to tell the truth, I had no idea who to ask about it until now."

Longarm shrugged and tersely explained, "They say Cherokee from the hills of northwest Georgia and east Tennessee used to dredge freshwater pearls before our kind made the first big gold strike north of Mexico in the Georgia hill country, back in the '30's before anybody'd ever heard of Sutter's Mill or Cherry Creek. So lots of local Cherokee took part in that first big gold rush, and lots of 'em learned a lot about mining gold."

The somewhat older Ash Woodside said, "Everyone in Colorado knows the first Colorado color was struck by the Cherokee Ralston brothers, and worked more serious by that Cherokee Baptist congregation where Cherry Creek runs unto the South Platte—right over yonder in Denver, for Pete's sake. I thought we were looking for that white gal who fingered this very post office for a fucking robbery, dad blast her unfashionable spring wardrobe!"

Longarm smiled sheepishly and said, "My boss, Marshal Vail, has encouraged my cravings for useless information. But you're right and let's see if I have all three women straight."

"*Three* women? I thought we were talking about *two*!" the postmaster said.

Longarm answered, "Three. Two local widow women coming in to *cash* money orders, and that strange gal coming in to *send* one. I know it's a tad confounding. That may have been premeditated. I'd like you to sort them out in the order you waited on them, Mr. Woodside."

Undersheriff Babcock suggested, "You ought to do as

he says, Ash. He catches crooks with his eliminating ways!"

Woodside thought before he declared, "The Widow Tenkiller came in first, before either of the others. Her envelope from the Indian Territory was in her delivery box in the back."

"You don't deliver mail to the homes in town?" asked Longarm.

Woodside shrugged and replied, "This ain't Paris, London, or even Denver, and I only have one clerk helping me. He wasn't here during the robbery because as a matter of fact he was out delivering the afternoon business mail up and down Main Street. We don't have the manpower to traipse up and down the slopes with personal letters to housewives. Elvira Tenkiller comes here to see if we're holding any mail for her. That afternoon we were. She opened it on yonder counter, and when she saw it was a postal money order I cashed it then and there for her, and she left as that mining man, Dick Trevor, came in to buy some stamps and post some letters all the way to England. Then that mousy gal I'd never seen before came in to buy a money order, and I was waiting on her when old Widow Strake came in to cash her own money order and—all right, I had my hands full, with the safe unlocked, when those masked men barged in and threw down on all of us!"

Longarm said, "I've got it pictured better now. Before it gets too late I'd better nip back to the Western Union to wire Saint Lou about them other folks named French over by the stockyards. Then I can drop by that local address she gave, 27 Mine Road, to see if there's really such an address and whether anyone's still up there or not."

Undersheriff Babcock marveled, "Did you see him do that without looking at his notebook? *I'd* drygulch him too if he was scouting *my* backtrail! How do you do that, old son? Do you have one of them photographing memories?"

Longarm modestly replied, "It ain't that tough to remember two-digit numbers, and you ain't got but five streets with names in this town, no offense. Mine Road would start just north of the stage depot and run up to the sheds and adit of your Mulligan mine, right?''

Both local men nodded. Babcock said, ''That's Mine Road. Ain't all that many private homes along Mine Road, now that you mention it. They haul the concentrated silver chloride down Mine Road to our north-south Main Street and wagon trace to the smelters and rail spur up to the county seat.''

Longarm allowed he'd best get cracking, but waited politely while Ash Woodside locked up and that deputy posted by the door said something to Undersheriff Babcock about a card game getting tense.

Longarm wasn't surprised when the older lawman allowed he'd walk Ash home and mayhaps see him around town later on. Longarm felt no need for an escort to the Western Union on a work night with the one main street nearly deserted under a now-star-spangled Rocky Mountain sky. How deserted the streets of Mulligan really were didn't hit him until he'd sent his wires and retraced his steps to the intersection of Main and Mine Road, to stare thoughtfully up the much darker thoroughfare, where nary a streetlamp and only a few pinpoints of any sort of light showed any signs of human habitation at all.

He strode up the cinder walk to pause in the shadows of a lumberyard fence and stare back the way he'd just come for what only felt like a million years.

Somewhere in the distance a tinkling piano was either playing ''Lorena'' or ''Aura Lee.'' It was hard to tell at any distance when a piano needed tuning. ''Lorena'' could drift into ''I'll Take You Home Again, Kathleen,'' if the piano player lost the thread after only a couple of beers.

Nobody seemed to be following him in the dark. He'd already been fairly sure that if the one who'd gotten away had ridden back to the settlement of Mulligan, he'd done so to lie low.

Longarm moved along until he found a doorway close

to the cinder sidewalk with a big gilt 18 outlined against its frosted door glass by a dim lamp lit inside. That meant odd numbers would be on the far side and starting from Main Street.

He was glad. It would have been tougher in the dark if the street numbers had commenced with the low numbers up near the silver mine. But as it was, he only had to count the dark masses on either side of the wide and deeply rutted road until, unless he was missing something, that four-story frame with a lamplit dormer window glowing from one flank of its hipped roof had to be the place.

Longarm crossed over quietly, noting there seemed to be another lamp lit deep in the bowels of the parlor floor, barely lighting up the bay windows to either side of the front door at the top of the veranda steps. There was a whole slew of cast-iron hitching posts lined up out front of the gated picket fence. The fence was backed by a greenup growth of pungent fern-leafed yarrow. When he opened the groaning gate and moved along the brick walk, it smelled as if he was entering an herb shop. They had creeping thyme instead of grass by way of a lawn, and the foundation plants along the base of the veranda smelled like garlic, chives, garden sage, oregano, and such. Longarm suspected somebody on the premises enjoyed cooking, or hated deer. Any gardening done in the foothills of the Front Range attracted its share of night-stalking mule deer, who'd nibble most anything that didn't smell awful to a deer.

Standing at the foot of the steps in the pungent starlight, he felt undecided about his next move. It was getting late to call at a private residence. But the place seemed a tad large for one family, and he'd have taken it for a rooming house if he hadn't been told in town that their Drover's Rest was the only such place in Mulligan.

Gazing about, he decided, "It can't be a card house or whorehouse. This early in the evening, neither would be *this* quiet, even on a work night."

He decided to come back in the morning and see whether

anyone there had ever heard of a Mildred French in any capacity. But as he turned to go back and creak that gate open some more, a familiar voice called out to him, "Custis! Where are you going? Weren't you here to visit with us?"

He turned to see three female figures peering out at him from one of those bay windows, and had to laugh as everything fell in place so naturally.

By the time he'd mounted the steps, Portia Parkhurst had come to the front door to open it and let him in, saying, "We heard about the gunfight you had on your way from Denver, you poor thing! Have you found out who they were yet?"

As he followed her into a dimly lit but impressive hallway, Longarm replied, "With any luck they've brought the one loser in from the open range. The other got away clean. Who's been growing all them herbs, and do you know if they've planted any anise or licorice root?"

Portia blinked in surprise and replied, "I have no idea. The late Madame Velvet seems to have been quite a gardener in her day. I suppose fading lovelies like to surround themselves with beauty. Anise is that purple flower that smells like licorice, right? Let's go on into the parlor and meet the Gilliam girls while you tell us why you're looking for licorice in their garden, for heaven's sake!"

They did. Longarm was mildly and pleasantly surprised to discover the two Kansas spinsters were well preserved full-figured ladies of a certain age who didn't seem as coy and uncomfortable around male callers as he'd pictured them.

That was the trouble with picturing folks before you laid eyes on them. Cynthia Gilliam was the older of the two sisters and the namesake of her notorious aunt, Madame Velvet née Cynthia Gilliam before she'd gone wrong. This Cynthia confided early on that some called her Cyn, pronounced Sin, and warned him not to get any ideas about that because it had been her father's notion, not her own, to name her after an older sister who hadn't gone wrong yet.

Longarm had met another Cynthia, pronounced Sin, a spell back. She'd been an officer's wife who'd told everyone not to get the notion her name meant anything. Then she'd sinned every chance she'd gotten with most anything in pants.

The younger sister, Cordelia, was less forward. But both of them had ash-blond hair and neither could be described as mousy, in or out of those summer-weight gingham frocks in the same lime-green and white checks. Cordelia went out to the kitchen to rustle up some coffee and cake, while Portia explained they'd been talking about that nineteen-volume diary that was up in the dormer room where Madama Velver had passed away. That was what well-brought-up Victorian ladies called dying, passing away.

Longarm said he was frankly more interested in mousy gals calling themselves Mildred French and giving 27 Mine Road as their current mailing address.

Cyn Gilliam told him they'd evicted all the "working girls" who hadn't already lit out for greener pastures by the time they'd gotten out west from Wichita to claim their inheritance. Her kid sister backed her story as they all shared the coffee and cake.

Portia suggested there might be some names in the diary of soiled doves who'd have call to come up with such an address in a hurry. Longarm allowed it was worth a try before he'd thought that all the way through.

He had second thoughts when Cyn clapped her hands and declared, "Then it's settled, ah, Custis. We'll put you up for the night in our late aunt's room, with all those pages she wrote, and you can go over them to your heart's content. Doesn't that sound like fun?"

To which Longarm could only reply, "Well, it sounds like something I ought to try, and I've always enjoyed reading in bed. But to tell the pure truth, I've seldom turned in with any nineteen volumes of anything!"

Chapter 8

It was still a tad early for bedtime, even in a mountain town too far from civilization to rate its own mail delivery or police force. So Longarm was saved from feeling like Tom Sawyer being sent to bed early by three Aunty Pollys when Cyn Gilliam suggested a grand tour of the premises.

As the four of them wandered the maze by candlelight, Longarm saw why the three women seemed anxious for a man with a six-gun to stay the night. They told him they'd brought an elderly serving couple west from Kansas with them, but the gardener-handyman cum coachman and his housekeeping wife had been quartered above the carriage house out back, and so the main house lay empty as a tomb, or at any rate, an empty house of ill repute, with cobwebs already commencing to form in many a dark corner and odd smells hanging in many a closed and shuttered room.

Longarm sniffed in vain for the odor of licorice. Some of the gals and their clients had smelled mighty odd. But he detected no licorice amid the faint fumes of jasmine, tuberose, violet water, and stale body odors haunting the former scenes of fun.

Asking occasional questions but mostly listening, Longarm learned that some of the whores who'd worked there had started to drift off well before Madame Velvet had died. For neither the fading health of the madam nor the fading fortunes of a skimmed-off lode encouraged the boom-time brawls a lady of adventure got rich off.

The two sisters from Kansas didn't know as much about mining as a Colorado-based lawyer, and Portia didn't know as much about mining as he did. So Longarm wound up explaining to them how your average strike played out from the Rockies to the Sierra Nevadas, where something awesome long ago had accordion-pleated the North American continent in a series of north-south-trending basins and ranges.

Where the bedrock rose high in rocky-jumble ridges or volcanic plugs, witches' brews of hot acid-waters had filled the cracks or pores of granite basement rock, for the most part, with chlorides, florides, sulfides, and such of most every metal known to man, save for the odd exception of platinum and tin in the American West. The metallic ores settled out of the hellish mixtures at different temperatures, the way alcohol, water, and poisonous fusel oils separated in a moonshine still. In the Rockies you tended to find raw gold closer to the surface, and often washed out of the bedrock as placer color a man could pan for while squatting in a creek. Deeper in the bedrock, metallic gold gave way to some gold and even more silver salts a greenhorn could take for no more than discoloration. Silver Dollar Tabor over in Leadville had been a canny Scotch grubstaker who'd realized the blue-black stuff most were just shoveling out of the way was high-grade silver chloride. So that was how old Hob Tabor got to be Senator Silver Dollar Tabor.

As you mined ever deeper, silver salts gave way to "associated" metals such as lead, zinc, or if you were lucky, copper. Although an "association" of copper and gold in another blend of sulfides was a lot more likely, and iron was usually no more than a widespread red discoloration, spread too thin to be worth mining.

The mother lode struck by the long-gone Mulligan had

been mined to the stage where a steady modest profit could be made by the one mine left, directly up Mine Road, blasting and mucking medium-grade lead-zinc-silver chloride single-shift, with the slow but steady hardrock crews drawing three dollars a shift and nothing all that exciting having happened in recent memory, or expected to happen. So the slick four-to-five-dollar specialists, usually single and always well heeled, had drifted on to greener pastures, followed by more ambitious whores and gamblers, by the time Madame Velvet had first been to Doc Maytag about her indigestion and chest pains. Most of those left had left on their own after Madame Velvet's funeral. The few pathetic old whores who'd wanted to hang on had been bought out at Portia's suggestion, and nobody knew or cared where they'd wound up with their small amounts of traveling and drinking money.

Longarm filed it away without comment that the Kansas spinsters had come west with the pocket jingle for at least a good female lawyer, and the sense to see that old whores with no ambition could be paid off cheaper than the court costs of formal evictions might have run by the time you went all the way up to the county seat for the papers and paid off the sheriff's department for serving and enforcing them. Longarm caught himself showing interest in whatever they'd done with their holdings back in Wichita. But he had enough on his plate with the mission he was on for Uncle Sam. So he didn't get into it when the younger and shyer Cordelia said they were hoping to turn their old Colorado whorehouse into a resort hotel.

It was her older and bolder sister, Cyn, who joshed that there was barely enough business for the one hotel that was already in business closer to the stage depot and post office. She was the one who seemed to think the family fortune now lay in those nineteen volumes of the late Madame Velvet's diary. Longarm shot Portia a warning look that shut her up before she could go on about having wanted a lawman's views on such a juicy version of early Colorado history.

They had hot chocolate and more cake out in the kitchen, and then the two sisters put Longarm to bed while Portia headed for her own guest room on the floor below. They didn't look at one another as they parted company on that landing. Longarm figured old Portia knew the way and it was up to her. Men who went sneaking around late at night to discover they weren't really welcome could wind up looking dumb as a mouse in a milk bucket.

As they led him into a cozy dormer room that smelled of scented candle wax, lavender sachet, and clean old woman, Cyn seemed to think he'd want to know that her aunt had been found dead at that writing desk, not in the big feather bed near the window. Those leather-bound stationery-store diary volumes she'd been keeping were lined up in the order written along a wall shelf above the writing table. It was flutter-lashed Codelia who placed the ewer of fresh water and some gingersnaps on the lamp table and shyly but sort of slyly kicked the chamber pot under the bed to let him know it was there for him. He'd already figured he could always piss out the window if he had to. Well-brought-up ladies and gents in an age of iron and steam with the art of plumbing in its infancy had lots of ways to exchange such information without ever letting on they knew Queen Victoria or anyone else ever took a piss.

Somewhere in the night a clock was striking ten as the Gilliam sisters told him their regular housekeeper would be serving breakfast at six in the morning and giggled out, leaving him alone up there with the one coal-oil lamp burning by the head of the bed.

Longarm moved over to the door, saw there was no bolt, and sighed, "Well, they said they *found* the old lady dead up here. Nothing was said about busting in. So let's hope they have sense to lock up down below."

He hung his six-gun at the head of the bed and unhooked

his derringer to wedge it between the mattress and the bed-board before he undressed and took a couple of volumes of Madame Velvet's diary to bed with him.

It didn't take long to see what Portia was worried about.

It was all very well for an old whore to say General Bill Larimer and old Ned Wynkoop had led gold hunters out from Kansas to grab a lot of land, threaten one another's lives, and wind up having streets in Denver named after them. It was another thing entirely to imply that either the dapper, well-educated militiaman Larimer or the buckskin-clad brawler Ned Wynkoop had known gals like the younger Madame Velvet in the biblical sense while they were feuding, fussing, and shrewdly naming the sprawl along Cherry Creek after old Jim Denver, the governor of a then-much-bigger Kansas Territory.

Almost all of them were there, whether mentioned as casual patrons of the liquor bar downstairs, or as having more wicked and sometimes just plain disgusting fun with total strangers called Snake Hips Sue, Hot Lips Francine, or the ever popular India Rubber Gal. Longarm saw to his dismay that Madame Velvet had given away the real name and family background of the saintly Miss Silver Heels, the Angel of the South Park!

Miss Silver Heels, a dance hall gal so called for the high silver heels of her high-button shoes, had put on more clothes and pitched in to help when a winter outbreak of the smallpox had swept the remote mining camp called Buckskin Joe. Serving soup and tender care to the dead and dying through a bleak and bitter winter, Miss Silver Heels had vanished with the spring. So they'd named a nearby peak Mount Silver Heels in her honor, and Longarm, for one, held it was nobody's business whether she'd left the gold fields forever after losing her looks to the smallpox, or married up with one of her patients after he'd struck it rich to make a society lady out of her.

The diary of Madame Velvet didn't say. Like everyone else around the South Park at the time, Madame Velvet had only been told how the boys had taken up a collection for Miss Silver Heels as the columbines bloomed and traipsed up to her cabin with it, only to find her cabin deserted and the never-to-be-forgotten Miss Silver Heels gone like the snows of yesteryear.

Madame Velvet cited other legendary women of an earlier West, along with a lot more Longarm had never heard of, since the working life of your average high country whore wasn't all that long. But Longarm was able to spot many a pioneer in pants who'd likely never known he was being recorded for posterity as a wild and woolly whorehouse visitor in his younger days.

No punches were pulled as Madame Velvet described the memorable Mother-Lode Gregory as he'd sobbed to the Indian Rubber Gal how he missed his wife and kids back in Georgia.

She'd recorded how Uncle Dick Wooten from Virginia had celebrated the opening of his trading post along Cherry Creek by smashing in the head of a cask of Taos lightning and getting everyone for miles around dead drunk for free. Longarm wasn't sure the current kith and kin of Bill Byers would enjoy reading how the now-respectable William Byers had started publishing the *Rocky Mountain News* in the loft above Uncle Dick's brawling trading post either, but there it was.

She had nothing dirty to say about Kit Carson's cousin, the squaw man George Jackson, who'd first panned color on the far slope of the Front Range in the hot mineral waters of Idaho Springs. But the current high-toned Jackson clan would hardly be thrilled to be cited at all.

Other entries in those earlier volumes told of other now-respected pioneers in more lurid detail. Longarm whistled softly when he came to a Civil War hero who'd liked to put on a dress and serve the customers as one of the girls. Pay-for-pleasure palaces could provide such other services as spankings, shit smearings, and in the case of one steady customer with the gold dust to spend, a mighty involved perversion where he'd put his old dick in a live goose, with its head up inside a lively whore, with the three of them wiggling and jiggling a lot until the suffocating goose was dead.

Madame Velvet allowed she'd found the experience too distasteful for the money. Longarm found it distasteful and sort of scary to think that the then-young pervert was now a big mining mogul and a national political figure. Longarm didn't think it would be wise to expose some of the other current bigwigs as erstwhile avid customers of Madame Velvet who'd liked things a lot of gents found disgusting or just plain silly. Had he not known Madame Velvet to have been a notorious boomtown whore, Longarm might have suspected her diary was the product of a sick imagination. He'd long suspected the diaries of Casanova and the raving of the Marquis de Sade were total bullshit produced by the wishful thinking of jerk-off artists. Longarm had found, as a man of some experience, that most folks just didn't act the way Casanova or de Sade had their devoted love slaves acting.

But what the hell, he'd never worked in a whorehouse, and even if Madame Velvet had indulged in some wishful thinking, she'd still used a lot of real names of still-living gents who were likely to get sore as hell if any of this shit got out!

As that distant clock struck again, Longarm set the dirty diary to the side, trimmed the lamp, and settled down to get some sleep, hoping he wouldn't dream about fucking a goose with its head up the skirts of Queen Victoria. The trouble with hearing or reading about a really wild sex act was that even when it made you sort of curious, there was seldom any uncomplicated way to explore further. Wondering what it might be like to fornicate with an Eskimo, an African pygmy, or even an elk seemed a waste of time as soon as you considered how much trouble you'd have to go to just getting into position.

Longarm chuckled and snuggled down into the soft

feather mattress with his eyes closed, deciding, "You'd probably wind up laughing too hard to get it up!"

Then he stiffened, naked under the covers, as he heard the snicker of a door latch turning in the dark.

Pretending to yawn in his sleep, Longarm got hold of his double derringer and covered the doorway from under the bed quilt as he waited with slitted eyes until, sure enough, a pale ghostly form in a nightgown came drifting over to whisper, "Custis? Are you asleep?"

"Not hardly. I was about to start without you!" he whispered back as he put his derringer away and made room for Portia's smaller frame in the ample feather bed.

Then they were all over one another, locked in a passionate embrace inspired, on his part at least, by those hours in the saddle and all that dirty reading since last he'd been doing anything half so fine with Miss Bubbles almost twelve hours earlier.

Miss Bubbles had been built fuller than most gals, hence the name. But he hadn't been in the leaner Portia Parkhurst for a spell, and so her flatter chest didn't feel flat enough to worry a man as he rolled atop her to wedge a pillow under her leaner hips before he entered her the way he knew she liked it.

As he did so, she hissed, "Oooh! Yesss! I was so afraid we wouldn't get the chance to do this tonight, darling!"

Longarm started moving in her, slow at first, because he knew she liked to start out almost casual and build up to a stampede off the cliff into the depths of desire, as she'd put it one time.

So he kissed the side of her throat and said, "If we hadn't done this here, you'd have doubtless found an excuse to get a room in that Drover's Rest the way I'd expected. You were right about that diary Miss Cyn wants to publish. We're going to have to convince her it's too dangerous to expose rich and powerful men as total degenerates."

She said out loud, "I told Cyn so. I told her we were

both likely to wind up dead if word about Aunt Cynthia's diary ever got out.''

Longarm stopped in mid-stroke, kissed her again in the dark, and cautiously ventured, ''Miss Cordelia?''

''Who did you think I was?'' asked the demure Miss Cordelia Gilliam. ''My poor frigid sister or that pathetic old maid Portia Parkhurst?''

Chapter 9

It might have sounded rude as well as stupid to ask a naked lady why she'd slipped out of her nightgown and into bed with a grown man in the middle of the night. So a good time was had by all until the two of them had come more than once and they were sharing a smoke, propped up against the bedboard with the pillows piled behind his back instead of under her ass.

The little ash-blonde's voice sounded more husky than shy as she said, "That was lovely. I came three times. How many times do you think anyone's ever come in this very bed, Custis?"

Longarm had noticed when he'd lit the cheroot how her usually shy and fluttering eyes had glowed wickedly by matchlight. He told her calmly, "Hard to say. Beds don't talk. I doubt your aunt entertained gentlemen callers up here in her private quarters. But she might have played with herself now and again."

Cordelia giggled, sounding dirty, and asked if he was suggesting even "that sort of woman" abused herself alone in bed.

Longarm shrugged the bare shoulder her blond head was snuggled against as he replied, "Nobody would have to abuse themselves if they *weren't* alone in bed. They say somebody asked the prophet Mohammed, or mayhaps it was Confucius, whether playing with yourself was a sin or not. He told them not to pester him with such dumb questions when it was a simple fact that nine out of ten people played with themselves and that tenth one was a big fibber.''

She insisted, ''I know how hard it can be to resist the temptation, but a bad girl like Auntie Cynthia, who must have gone all the way with more men than she could have possibly remembered?''

Longarm smiled thinly and assured her, ''With birds too, according to her diary. It ain't true that ladies in her line of work have no feelings down yonder. They just don't take them as serious as most women, one way or the other. I have it on good authority that after a hard night in the saddle with the herd in town and total contempt in their loins for the kid cowboys poking them, many a trail-town hooker unwinds a lot of stored-up distaste with the help of another gal, her own hand, or any of several bedtime toys sold in secret in novelty shops.''

Cordelia chuckled fondly and said, ''Oh, I see you got to that entry about her putting on that show at a stag party with that crazy Chinese invention.''

To which Longarm was forced to reply, ''Not hardly. I only skimmed through the first few volumes before she seemed to be repeating herself. You say she entertained a Chinese stag party? A stunt like that could get a white hooker sent to jail out on Frisco Bay.''

The dead whore's niece said, ''It wasn't a Chinese stag party, silly. It was over in Leadville to celebrate the appointment to West Point of an illiterate mining man's oldest boy. The Chinese love-tool she demonstrated, as near as I can picture it, seems to have been a sort of glass violin.''

She moved Longarm's free hand to her own warm fuzzy lips as she went on. ''The woman playing a solo on it inserts the smooth glass neck of the instrument up inside her, like a dildo. Then she, or a friend, draws a regular violin bow back and forth over the glass bowl between her open thighs to, well, make the whole thing hum and tingle while she, or a friend, moves the shaft in and out of her.''

Longarm took a thoughtful drag on his cheroot and decided, ''You're right. It's hard to picture. Not the queer glass fiddle. Such a thrill as any gal might get out of it. Did your aunt's diary say whether she cottoned to such fiddle-faddle or not?''

Cordelia told him, ''She said it made her feel silly. Then all those mining men at the stag party took turns raping her, if rape is exactly how you'd define it, and she says that felt more normal.''

Longarm observed that some gals found building up to it almost as much fun. Cordelia said, ''I just like to fuck. I don't see how I could ever become a whore like Aunt Cynthia. I like to decide on a man and then fuck him *my* way. I'd feel stupid sitting around and waiting for some man to come in and decide he wanted to fuck me, as if he was ordering a meal. It was boring enough waiting for customers to come in to our notions shop back in Wichita. But everyone to her own taste, say I, and some of the men at that stag party went on to become rich and famous. Have you gotten to the part about the copper king who had Aunt Cynthia shove that same glass shaft up his rear end and play it for *him* while he played with *himself*?''

Longarm made a wry face and replied, ''Not hardly. It would take a good three or four nights to read all nineteen volumes, and I for one have better things to spend the time on.''

He took another thoughtful drag on his smoke and added with a sad philosophical sigh, ''It hardly seems fair. The poor old gal seems to have wasted close to twenty years worth of evening musings on her dirty diary, and if you put your mind to it you could read it all in less than nineteen hours. Sort of makes you wonder why anybody would bother with keeping a diary, don't it?''

Cordelia said, ''Oh, I don't know. I kept a diary for a

while when I was still in school. It's not as if you have to buckle down like a novelist and write hundreds of pages all at once. My average entry only took me a few minutes a night. But of course, my average entry was a lot shorter. Twelve-year-old virgins don't really have a lot to write about in their diaries.''

Longarm asked how come she'd given the notion up.

She said, "I just told you. The same reason most young virgins lose interest in keeping diaries, once they're no longer young virgins. By the time I was thirteen I saw nothing I'd recorded for the ages was ever going to be read by the ages. So I just stopped, and it was just as well, because I lost my cherry the summer I turned fifteen, and that marvelous night of the Harvest Moon Hayride would have never been safe to put down on paper!''

She fondled his limp manhood as she coyly added, "His wasn't this big, and Lord knows he didn't know how to use it as well, but it was big enough and he used it well enough to satisfy any fifteen-year-old student. He was my English Literature teacher, you see, and even though his wife didn't understand him, he'd been married long enough to know how it was done.''

Longarm grimaced and said, "I suspect his wife understood him way better than he did. But had he left you chaste, I'd have wound up all alone up here with all this romantic writing, so what the hell.''

She began to work it firmer as she purred, "Had I still been keeping a diary, I'd have wondered on paper how anyone could say I'd *lost* anything on that hayride. When you learn to swim or fly a kite, does anybody say you've *lost* anything? I was *proud* of myself, knowing I'd done something my older sister, Cyn, had never done. I felt *cleverer* sitting in school the next Monday, knowing only the married teacher, myself, and maybe that trashy Phillis Cafferty knew what it was like to come with a man instead of penny candle like a kid!''

He snubbed out the cheroot and reached down under the

covers to return the favor as she stroked him harder and calmly decided, "I'd never put down how I'm feeling right now on paper. What do you suppose drove poor old Aunt Cynthia to spell such things out in such detail? I know I'd never forget what it felt like if a poor tortured goose was drowning inside of me, and I'd never in this world want another soul to know I'd ever taken part in such crazy perversions!"

He removed her no-longer-needed hand and rolled atop her to slide it in right as he replied, "The total idiot helping you kill birds that way would still know, and allowing she spelled his name right, I reckon he'd be mighty chagrined to learn you and me both know what a perverse idiot he was in his gold-panning youth."

As they started loping up the rise together like old pals, he decided, "Your aunt might have worried about having to remember way more such romance than the rest of us. I've never hankered to list each and every lover I've ever . . . kissed, and Lord knows I've never had nigh as many lovers as even a beginner in your late aunt's trade. But from time to time, like most men, I've found myself alone with nothing at all better to do, so I try to add up how many gals I've ever . . . kissed."

She locked her ankles in the small of his back as she kept time with his thrusts, saying, "Up until now I've fucked seventeen different men, and naturally fucked most of them more than once. Can you tell?"

He thrust in and out judiciously before he replied in a mocking tone, "I would have made it at least twenty-one. My point is that any man just laying there, counting fondly on his fingers as he recalls good times and better times, catches himself skipping over someone and having to go back and start all over. It hardly seems you'd forget a hotel maid you almost got caught with, but there you are, counting that gal at the hotel in Cheyenne when you suddenly recall that *other* one you spent less time with in Casper, and so maybe someone who *really* had a lot to remember would have to keep written records. Don't ask me why a hooker would want to be certain she'd been fucked on a payday night by thirteen or fourteen drunks, but she must have had her own good reasons. The point is that she did it, and I agree with you and your lawyer, Miss Portia. Even submitting such a load of dynamite to some publisher like Edward Judson could stir up a whole lot of trouble for you ladies!''

Cordelia didn't seem to care until he'd made her come again. Then she held him tight and marveled, "You're incredible. Who is Edward Judson?"

Longarm said, "The sort of publisher who'd put out such a scandal-filled history of Colorado as your late aunt's diary. Knowing the way he works, he'd likely get you in more trouble with added details nobody ever put down. I've threatened him with bodily harm if he ever puts me in bed with Calamity Jane or has me killing Indian chiefs who never lived. Ted Judson's better known by a pen name, Ned Buntline. He made up the names Buffalo Bill and Wild Bill for other High Plains riders on better terms with him. He still pays Bill Cody drinking money to keep quiet about such dime novels as *Buffalo Bill, King of the Border Men*. I've no idea *what* he pays old Bill Cody. They say the play the two of them put on, *Scouts of the Plains,* lost money when the audience laughed at the wrong parts. But no matter what Judson or his ilk might be willing to pay for the rights to, say, a *Diary of Madame Velvet,* you ought to think twice before you accept a million dollars and a free passage to some far and distant land."

She said, "Let me get on top. Do you think such a publisher as this Edward Judson would have the nerve to market Auntie Cynthia's diary?"

As she lowered herself snugly on Longarm's semierection, he twitched it inside her and said, "He's been established as a publisher who knows no fear, or common sense. He's been married at least eight times and survived numerous gunfights, one in a Tennessee courthouse, where the charges against him were dismissed when the other party took three shots at him on the witness stand. He's killed at least one man, libeled hundreds in his scandal sheet, *Ned Buntline's Own,* and survived at least one lynching, so sure, he'd likely take a chance on the diary of another famous Western character. He still keeps writing about poor James Butler Hickok and Calamity Jane. They say he can churn out two hundred pages a day in longhand. So one danger I see from Judson or his sort of publisher is having your family treasure *stolen.* I'd make sure I sold it through some third party acting as your agent—if I sold it at all, that is. Could I get on top again? No offense, but if you like to talk and screw at the same time, you have to pay attention to your partner's needs."

She said she was sorry, and then sucked him off, and he managed to get some sleep after she'd made him promise he'd never tell and slipped out as quietly as she'd tiptoed in.

Next morning, he had ham and eggs with the others, served by the motherly housekeeper in the kitchen. Cordelia never looked at Longarm as she sat at the far end of the table, letting her lawyer and bolder-looking older sister do all the talking.

They both wanted to know what he thought of the diary of Madame Velvet. He said that from what he'd read, Madame Velvet had suffered an active life or a vivid imagination, and that in any case a lot of powerful men, or their kith and kin in the case of some dead war heroes and enshrined founding fathers, were sure to be sore as all getout. He said, "The burden of proof is on the accuser in a court of law, but on the accused in the court of public opinion. So many a powerful gent with friends in high places might not want to go through formal legal proceedings, whether guilty as charged by Madame Velvet or not!"

Portia Parkhurst, Attorney at Law, who kept smiling at Longarm as if butter wouldn't melt in her mouth, asked if he'd wondered too how much of Madame Velvet's recorded misadventures were true. When both the dead woman's nieces shot her stricken looks, Portia said, "As your legal advisor, I have to say that has to be considered. Custis here would know more about the way his kind might act liquored up around women none of us would ever associate with. But speaking as a woman who's never been involved in such wild parties, I still find some of those wild parties your older kinswoman describes a bit . . . improbable."

Longarm didn't think she wanted him to tell about that time they'd discovered, back in Denver, that some of the positions illustrated in the forbidden Hindu Kama Sutra, published with a plain brown cover, were just plain impossible.

He repeated that it didn't matter, and added, "We'll never know why Madame Velvet has certain pillars of Colorado society behaving in their younger days like randy freaks. The point is that if I were you young ladies, I'd just unload this property at the best price possible and hold off on publishing the diary of Madame Velvet for now. Today it's safe to speculate on whether Queen Elizabeth was really a virgin queen or how much Frederick the Great liked young boys. But saying as much whilst either was alive and in power could have taken fifty years or more off one's life."

The older Gilliam sister, Cyn, was still bitching about how little an empty whorehouse was worth in a town that was dying on the vine when the beefy old cuss who mostly worked out back came in to tell Longarm he was wanted at Doc Maytag's for that inquest.

So Longarm drained his cup, excused himself from the table, and told the ladies they'd talk about their own problems later, once he'd tended to more urgent chores.

They made him promise to come back. That was easy enough. He wanted to get Portia alone long enough to find out whether she'd been too shy to sneak upstairs to him, too sore at him to want to, or whether she and the deceptive

72

Cordelia had made a sneaky deal about him. One thing he'd learned about the unfair sex, long before he'd read that dirty diary, was that women could talk dirtier about men in private than most men could imagine.

Chapter 10

The red-faced, beer-bellied Doc Maytag had performed the autopsy in the cellar of his drugstore. A less than formal official inquest was held at a corner table in the Chloride Saloon across the street. Aside from Longarm, Undersheriff Babcock, and the druggist cum deputy coroner himself, they'd been joined at and about the table by some local stockmen, the foreman of the mining company's small private police force, and apparently any regular at the Chloride who wanted to listen in.

Undersheriff Babcock triumphantly waved a wanted flier and some typed-up sheets of onionskin as he crowed that he'd been doing some of that eliminating himself.

Longarm and the others had to agree when Babcock chortled, "Many a man has a scarred upper lip. Many a man has a rose growing round a cross tattooed on his left forearm. Many a man has an old bullet scar in his right thigh. But put them all together and they spell Pecos Tim Sheehan, wanted for murder in San Antone and reputed to have done in many another man with a buffalo gun for a fee."

Doc Maytag dryly observed, "It was that fresher bullet wound over the heart that ended his career as a hired gun.

Whatever happened to his Sharps .50-170 he was aiming your way, Deputy Long?''

Longarm soberly replied, "He left it up on the hogback and the licorice-eating son of a bitch who got away must have taken it with him. But when you study on it, *that's* a distinguishing feature someone might connect to a stranger, or some good old boy, riding in ahead of me yesterday evening.''

Undersheriff Babcock said the trouble with that notion was that nobody he'd canvassed recalled *anybody* riding hard into town just ahead of the federal law.

Longarm shrugged and suggested, "We'd best ask around some more then. Or mayhaps the cuss circled wide to ride in from a more innocent-looking direction—say, the coach road south from Golden?''

Babcock looked injured and replied, "Unless he never rid nowheres *near* Mulligan after you gave him one hell of a fright and left him alone on open range with night coming on.''

One of the men who grazed the surrounding hills volunteered, "You don't have to stick to no trail betwixt here and the county seat. You find plenty of grass and a little water all up and down these foothills, with nothing to bar your way. He'd have only needed to follow a dotted line of passes through the rimrocks if he'd wanted to beeline east to the Denver railroad yards. A natural temptation, but not a wise move with *you* betwixt him and Denver.''

Longarm had nothing further to contribute. So Doc Maytag asked him to sign one of the papers he was mailing up to Golden, and once Maytag had signed up the rest of his ad hoc panel, Longarm was free to go.

So he headed first for Levine's Creamery, just up the way on the same side of the street. Meyer Levine turned out to be an older man who'd doubtless been nibbling at his own wares, or had a real tempting cook for his woman. He had that all-over build of a sea lion, or an active overeater who moves about too much for the fat to settle in any particular place. He looked a few years older than Longarm, but hardly old enough to talk to a grown lawman as if Longarm attended that schoolhouse just up the same block. But Levine seemed a neighborly enough possible witness, and so Longarm assumed the candy store man had just gotten that way dealing with kids for penny candy. Schoolmarms were inclined to talk that way to a man, even dogstyle. Folks picked up the lingo of those they spent the most time with, which was likely why ladies crossed the street when they saw cowhands heading their way.

Meyer Levine confirmed he did indeed sell loose candy by the pound or less in those striped paper bags. When Longarm let him sniff the one recovered from the scene of that shoot-out, the expert on such subjects declared without hesitation, "Licorice toffee, imported from England, individually wrapped in lead foil and selling, retail, two for a penny. I tell my customers American licorice sticks are a better buy, but who listens? Some people think tobacco grows better in faraway Turkey than Virginia, but confidentially Kentucky tobacco is best."

Longarm said he was more interested in the sweet tooth of a suspect than his smoking habits. Admitting he'd never laid eyes on the rider who'd gotten away, Longarm said it was safe to say he'd looked like a run-of-the-mill rider, not wanting to stand out, packing a Big Fifty buffalo gun, which might have made him stand out.

Meyer Levine proved himself a man who thought on his feet as well by observing, "He'd have bought his imported licorice here *before* he had to ride away with his partner's rifle, and who's to say which one likes licorice?"

Longarm conceded the point, and described the one he'd shot.

The storekeeper thought before he replied, "*Nu,* a scar-faced oily stranger I'd remember. A scar-faced oily stranger I *don't* remember. I don't sell that much imported sweets of any flavor, and most of the *kinder* up the block buy licorice whips, not toffee, to begin with."

Then, as Longarm was about to thank him and turn away, the local authority on confections volunteered, "Wait! Cowboys buying imported licorice I don't remember. A young woman new in town with a craving for licorice I suddenly remember. I think she might be a new schoolteacher up the block. Like a schoolteacher she looked, and from the way she asked if we sold licorice, you'd have thought it was opium and she'd been told not to come home without it!"

Longarm cocked a brow to reply, "She well might have. What did this strange gal in a small town look like?"

"A mouse," Meyer Levine replied without hesitation. "Maybe at second glance not so bad, but at first glance, *oy*! My daughter Sarah is going through a stage and like a mop she wears her hair, but you know what? Next to that mousy stranger, my Sarah is groomed like the Princess of Wales on her way to a party. The mousy hair on the head of that mousy customer looked like a wig made out of spiderwebs or the fuzz balls you find under beds!"

Longarm said, "Maybe it was. We suspect those outlaws who robbed your post office had a woman described as mousy scouting ahead for the four of them. An outlaw shy about taking the point might well send a gal out to buy things for him, and a gal scouting a fancy brand of licorice for a moody gunslick might well have reasons for looking anxious. I have another witness on my list who might have seen that selfsame mousy gal on a less innocent errand. I'm looking for the house number of a widow woman called Elvira Tenkiller. I was hoping some of your shopkeepers might know her. She failed to put down her house number when she signed for a postal money order the night of that robbery. They were robbing the place at the time."

Meyer Levine said, "I know Elvira Tenkiller. My wife is a customer. I don't have her house number. But she runs her own dressmaking business over the stationery store just past that school. By my wife, she's a fine seamstress. By me, what can I tell you? Do I look like I'm in the market for a dress?''

Longarm laughed, bought a nickel's worth of gumdrops to show he was a sport, and headed up the walk to scout up Elvira Tenkiller.

Passing the whitewashed schoolhouse, he saw school was in session with the kids all inside. It was likely not a good idea to hand out gumdrops in a schoolyard to begin with. So he popped one in his mouth, tossed the small red and white bag on some horseshit in the gutter so it would be swept up, and moseyed on up to the sign he saw advertising stationery and office supplies.

When he got there, a smaller sign over a side door announced he'd find Elvira Tenkiller, Dressmaker and Seamstress, on the next floor.

He stared into the show window of the stationery store, not sure what he was looking for, and then went on up to canvass the Widow Tenkiller.

He found her alone in her dinky, clean, but cluttered dress shop, running a seam with her foot-powered Singer machine. As he showed her his badge and identification, she allowed she'd been expecting him, and got up from her sewing to put the coffee on a tiny potbelly in another corner. He'd been expecting someone more like Miss Minnehaha, even though he knew lots of Cherokee. Elvira Tenkiller looked more like a fashionable French lady who'd been out in the sun a lot without her parasol.

He wasn't surprised by her trim bodice and Dolly Varden skirts of summer-weight calico, printed to resemble blue willow chinaware, and most Indian gals kept their thick straight hair well groomed. But like a lot of Cherokee men and women, this young widow looked more Scotch-Irish than anything else.

She likely was. The late Chief Ross of the Cherokee Nation had been seven-eighths Scotch-Irish, descended from a long line of Scotch, Irish, and High Dutch traders who'd married into an important Cherokee clan and passed the business down to halfbreed sons who'd married a high-born Cherokee gal, or breed, in turn. He knew that Tenkiller was as high-toned a name among her Cherokee kin as Morgan or Vanderbilt might be to his own. But he didn't ask her for a rundown of her own family tree. He explained how Postmaster Woodside had said she'd been leaving about the same time as that mousy mystery woman should have been fixing to barge in ahead of those masked gunmen.

The far from mousy brunette breed nodded soberly and said, "I've already been over all of that with Undersheriff Babcock and those postal inspectors. I'm sorry to say so, but as I told them, I had cashed a money order from home and left the post office before it was robbed. I didn't see any strangers on Main Street that evening as I walked only as far as my corner and turned up the slope to the cabin the mining company has allowed me to go on renting. Those outlaws and their female accomplice must have approached from some other direction."

Longarm almost let her testimony stand. But that wasn't why they called him the best tracker out of the Denver District Court. Nodding politely, he suggested, "Try to remember anybody of the female persuasion you *knew* heading toward that post office as you were walking away from it."

She moved over by her stove to open a cupboard and rustle up some cups, saucers, and half a marble cake as she shook her head to tell him, "I don't think so. No, wait, now that you mention it *that* way, I think I *did* see one of Madame Velvet's soiled doves coming my way along the walk!"

Longarm asked, "Hadn't Madame Velvet passed away before the night of that holdup, Miss Elvira?"

She spread the chinaware on a tray and then shifted the tray to a dinky rosewood coffee table in front of a slip-covered love seat as she said, "I think so. I never met the notorious Madame Velvet. I suspect she thought she was too refined to patronize a squaw. But I made some Sunday-Go dresses for more than one of her fallen women, including the poor thing I passed in the gloaming the night of the robbery.''

Longarm suggested, ''Madame Velvet may have feared you might think you were too good for *her*, and squaw ain't a cruel word for a lady of Indian blood amongst Algonquin-speaking Arapaho, Cheyenne, and such. But you've *heard* all that. So let's talk about why you felt so sorry for this white gal *working* for Madame Velvet, Miss Elvira.''

The attractive well-groomed breed put the cake on the table and moved to see if the coffee had been rewarmed enough to serve as she told him, ''I assumed she'd fallen on hard times since last I'd outfitted her in a fall riding habit. I'd forgotten vague things I'd heard about that house of ill repute closing down. So it seemed to me, at first glance, she'd taken to strong drink and sleeping in gutters. She was all musty and dusty, and Lord knows what she'd done with her hair. I'd always suspected she used henna rinse, but that evening, as she came along the walk with a dirty face and a head of hair that looked more like a dust mop that needed a shaking, I was so embarrassed for her that I looked the other way as we passed. It was only later that I realized she might have felt I was snubbing her!''

As she poured the coffee, Longarm said, ''I've reason to suspect she was hoping you didn't recognize her. That place she used to work ain't in her line of work no more. The new owners are hoping to do something more wholesome with the property. But such houses of ill repute tend to be way stations along the owlhoot trail some outlaws ride, not wanting to register in regular hotels or boarding-houses and knowing they're likely to be questioned if they camp out in the open near a town.''

As she cut some cake, Elvira asked if he thought those four robbers had been staying with that poor messed-up thing at Madame Velvet's.

Longarm said, "One or more of 'em might have met her there and . . . formed an attachment. It's sad but true that many such gals are sort of hoping a Prince Charming will come along to take them away from such tedious employment and install them in a castle in the sky, or at least a place they can call their own along the owlhoot trail."

He tasted some of her marble cake to be polite. It wasn't as stale and her coffee wasn't as bad as he'd feared. So he told her how great they both tasted, and explained, "I have it on good authority that some of Madame Velvet's more ambitious employees had already lit out before a sick old lady could die and leave the business to some kin who were not in her business. Tell me some more about the mining company renting cabins to folks who ain't on the company payroll, no offense. I ain't just being nosy. One of Madame Velvet's gals moving into her own private quarters, with room to spare for, say, four others, would explain a lot of what we've been having a lot of trouble explaining!"

So she told him in detail how the mine owners who'd built most of Mulligan had allowed her to stay on after her late husband, a blaster, had made a fatal mistake with 60 percent DuPont. She didn't know if just anybody could rent a company cabin since they'd laid off the night shift and so many families had moved away.

He said he'd ask, politely declined second helpings, and was on his way while the morning was still young. He hadn't had a chance to shower, shave, or change his underwear after that interesting night in the bed of Madame Velvet. So he dropped by the Drover's Rest to do so while he had the spare time.

On his way past the desk with his room key still in his pocket, he was called over by the desk clerk, who handed him a white envelope he said a lady had dropped off earlier.

The envelope was blank. There was nothing inside. Not even a blank sheet of paper. Longarm said, "I don't get it. You say a lady asked you to pass this on to me?"

The clerk said, "Around breakfast time with the lobby

crowded and me busy juggling keys for less experienced travelers. She never said who she was or what she might be to you. She just asked if you were staying here, and when I said you were, she handed me this envelope for you and left.''

Longarm nodded and said, ''I'm commencing to see the light. What did my mysterious caller look like?''

The clerk said, ''Like I said, I was busy and she wasn't pretty nor ugly enough to describe as anything but sort of *mousy*. Does that call anyone you know to mind?''

Chapter 11

The surface workings and supervisory shed of the Mulligan Mine were clustered around the adit leading steeply into the main shaft. But of course their company business offices, like their company store, were along the one main street of the company town they'd built.

He found the rental office over the company store, with an outside staircase going up to it along the side of the building facing south on an east-west alleyway. Upstairs, he was admitted into the comfortable office of their rental agent, and set down in a tufted leather chair with a cigar in one hand and a tumbler of bourbon and branch water in the other while he told the effusive rental agent with wavy hair to match his freshly laundered linen shirt what Mulligan Mines Incorporated could do for their Uncle Sam.

Longarm explained his simple line of questions, and the rental agent allowed he followed Longarm's drift. He said, "We've already had our company police scour the scattered empty cabins for prowlers and squatters. We caught a whole tribe of Gypsies living in empty miners' quarters on our Boulder County property. Nothing like that down here in Jefferson County, though. Say they left their ponies somewhere else. Four strange men and a gal or more would have been noticed by mining families still renting from us, and someone would have surely gossiped about a known hooker from Madame Velvet's whorehouse moving in next door!''

Longarm said, ''Be that as it may. Might you have been renting such cabins to anyone not directly connected with your mining operations?''

The rental agent didn't hesitate to nod and innocently reply, ''Sure. Those cabins were built to be rented for ten dollars a month, not to stand empty. This whole town will stand empty soon enough unless we hit another vein of high-grade chloride. Some lots platted in the beginning were set aside for others to build on and others did. But smaller businessmen and real-estate speculators can't afford to rent for much higher than ten dollars a month. So as the housing market in town has loosened up, others have approached us and, if I say so myself, we've been more than fair about renting at the same low rate to one and all.''

Longarm was too polite to say that renting at the going rate was good business but hardly more than fair. You gouged customers at the *beginning* of a gold rush, not when the bloom was fading from a lead and silver operation.

He said, ''That former hooker who seems to have been trying to alter her appearance was likely whoring under a phony name to begin with. But it's possible she gave such a name, or a different name than she used as a whore, to a dressmaker I was talking to earlier. What if you were to let me have a list of your company cabins currently being rented by folks neither working for nor married up with anyone working for you all directly?''

The rental agent said he could do better than that. One of those postal inspectors who'd been by earlier had asked the same questions about strangers holed up in a company town. So the company had typed up carbon-paper lists of all their tenants, with an X after the names of any not on the company payroll. As he rang for his stenography gal, he explained how Undersheriff Babcock's boys had already scanned the pages in vain for anyone not known around town. But Longarm allowed he'd still be much obliged, and when the gal brought the carbon copies in to him, he put them away with a nod of thanks and then rose to drain his glass, thank them both with handshakes, and be on his way with the Havana cigar gripped in his teeth and his afternoon undecided.

Since it was getting on toward noon, he knocked off for a bowl of chili con carne with oyster crackers. As he was mulling over all the desserts they had on display, he noticed they served marble cake. He ordered chocolate layer cake with his coffee, but headed back to where he'd had coffee and marble cake to see if Elvira Tenkiller could match up any of the names on the mining company's rent rolls with one or more of the whores she'd made dresses for. The widow of a company man had never said whether she recalled the given name of that one whore or not. But Longarm figured that if he ran a dressmaking business, he'd expect ladies ordering a dress to tell him who in blue blazes they might be. He felt sure *he'd* put their names down somewhere, at least until he'd been paid. So it was worth a try, and if she thought he was sparking her, that was her misfortune and none of his own. There was no law saying a gent couldn't call on a lady twice in the same day as long as he behaved like a gent both times.

Like most naturally active men, Longarm hated paperwork, and whether she hated it herself or kept business records in writing, the Widow Tenkiller could likely save him a lot of paperwork. For while there were hundreds of names on the lists he'd just gotten from that rental agent, and Madame Velvet appeared to have recorded the names of every whore who'd ever worked for her, along with the names of most every man who'd ever paid for their services, a small-town dressmaker could have only made so many dresses for so many whores.

So whether that mousy mystery woman had given a false name or not, once he had any names she might have given, along with those of other hookers who might have served

85

those same owlhoot riders, he'd be in a much better position to just skim the rent rolls and the more recent volumes of the diary of Madame Velvet for possible matchups. He knew he was looking for a petite white whore who'd likely looked better with her face washed and her hair combed, henna-rinsed or otherwise. The timing worked best if Madame Velvet had her leaving the premises just before her death, or still there when the Gilliam sisters took over. It was too much to hope for, but should he find the current home address of a fading flower the new owners had paid off through their lawyer, Portia, that post office robbery was as good as solved. A used-up whore, lacking the ambition to hang in there or move on to another boom, was a whore likely to spill her guts after a night or so in the Women's House of Detention with nothing to drink and a kindly lawman willing to make a deal with her before that *mean* lawman came back from the crapper.

There was a cordovan cow pony tethered in front of the stationery store under a double-rigged silver-mounted roper with a Mexican saddle blanket and a braided leather reata. He glanced idly through the front window of the stationery shop to see the old lady who ran it alone behind her counter, reading a book. So he moved up the stairs to Elvira Tenkiller's door on the balls of his feet, and quietly drew his .44-40 when he heard what sounded like a slap and the voice of Elvira sobbing, "How can I tell you what I don't know? I've never heard of your Valya Sick-Whatever! If I ever did any sewing for her, she gave me some other name!"

A rougher male voice insisted, "They call her Russian Val and she'd have that outlandish way of talking English no matter what name she gave you! Don't lie to me, you fucking squaw! What did you tell that lawman about Russian Val?"

The Cherokee dressmaker insisted, "Nothing! There was nothing to tell because he never asked! He never asked because I suspect neither one of us ever heard of any Russian gal!''

There came the sound of another slap, and Longarm made up his mind to chance it as he heard the poor gal's pathetic sobs. She was likely more scared than hurt. But no man could just stand there like a big-ass bird while a woman was being beaten on the far side of one thin door. So hoping he only had one woman-beater on the far side to deal with, Longarm was fixing to bust in when he heard another male voice ring out, ''That's enough for here and now. We'd better take her to the boss lady and let *her* decide. This one knows more than she's fixing to tell us, or she's really as dumb as she says. In either case, another woman knows more than we do about eating pussy or getting another one to tell the truth. Here, tie her wrists with this latigo and we'll just take her for a walk in the sunshine.''

The one who'd been pushing Elvira around suggested, ''Why don't *you* tie her wrists whilst I whip across the way and get my own pony?''

The one who seemed in charge snapped, ''Why don't you do as you're told for a change and save us all the clanking and creaking of your vast steam-powered brain? You don't ride off in broad daylight with a woman's skirts flapping betwixt two *horses,* you asshole! We leave our ponies be and *walk* her off up the slope as if the three of us are on our way home for a late dinner or early supper, see?''

The one who'd been meaner to Elvira snickered, ''Why can't we walk her home for a fuck party? Wouldn't you like to service two white men at the same time, you noble little savage?''

Longarm crawfished into the darker dead end of the upstairs landing as he figured a less risky way for Elvira Tenkiller. So neither of the tall men in Texas hats glanced his way as they popped out her doorway with the scared-skinny brunette wedged between them.

It was Elvira, rolling her big brown eyes all about in desperation, who spotted the tall dark figure of Longarm with his back to the wall, and it was Elvira, bless her, who never said shit as her captors spun her between them to face down the stairs with her hands lashed behind her back. Longarm took a deep breath as the three of them lined up with their backs to him, outlined by the daylight through the frosted glass far below, and let half of it out so his voice wouldn't crack as he yelled, "Unhand that woman and drop them guns or I'll shoot!"

Some folks just couldn't follow simple directions. The gal they'd been abducting dropped her shapely rump to the top step with her heels dug in stubbornly as one of them tried to hang on to her while the other yelled, "Oh, shit!" and whirled on the landing with his own six-gun in hand. So Longarm blew him off the landing to flop ass-over-teakettle down the stairs as limp as a wet dishrag, but a lot more thumpy and bumpy.

By this time Elvira had kicked the one trying to lift her dead weight in the shins, and so by the time Longarm put two hundred grains of lead through the space he'd been in, he too was thumping and bumping down the stairs, and yelling like hell besides.

Longarm moved in to hunker down by the wrist-bound dressmaker and haul her back on her rump on the landing until she was out of the line of any fire up the stairs. Then he rose to aim down the stairs through the haze of gun smoke fogging the stairwell, and pegged another shot at blurred outlines as at least one of them flung open the door to tear outside, even though he was yelling, "Don't shoot! I give up!"

Longarm fished out his pocketknife to drop it on the landing next to the wrist-bound gal, and shouted, "Get your hands in front of you by pressing your palms to the floor and hauling your rump back through the loop. I'll send help directly if I don't lose!"

By the time he'd said that much, he was halfway down

the stairs, not looking back. The one sprawled just inside the gaping doorway was dead or done for. Longarm skipped over him to tear out on the walk in a gunfighting crouch as the pony tethered out front fought its tether, wall-eyed and kicking up dust. More dust hung in the sunlight where another pony had been tied up across the way. As the street commenced to fill, Longarm yelled, "I'm the law! Which way did he ride?" and nobody answered. So Longarm legged it down to the first intersection to look both ways, as other townsfolk boiled out of doors shouting dumb questions and calling for some law and order.

Law and order first arrived in the person of a mining company man and one of the county deputies, from opposite directions. So Longarm yelled, "Stairwell next to the stationery store. One man down one to go for certain."

Then he ran back to see how Elvira Tenkiller was making out with his pocketknife and the corpse at the foot of her stairs. He had to elbow his way through the crowd gathering around the open doorway, where the one he'd nailed lay on his side staring out at them all as if they'd disturbed his rest. One hand seemed to be reaching for the five-shot Remington .45 out on the walk. A rivulet of blood was still oozing across the weathered planking toward it, as if some part of him meant to get to that damned gun one way or the other.

Longarm hunkered to gather up such evidence before anyone could take it for a souvenir. That was what some called anything they could steal from a dead man, a souvenir.

He found Elvira Tenkiller standing tall with her hands free at the top of the stairs. As she handed back his knife, she blathered something about owing him her virtue if not her life. She clung to his sleeves and pressed her head to his vest as she sobbed, "They were kidnapping me when you arrived out of nowhere! How can I ever thank you?"

He patted her back and replied, "Aw, mush, I didn't appear out of nowhere. I came back to ask for the names of those wicked women you made dresses for. I was listening outside when you told them you'd never heard of anyone called Russian Val. Was that the truth, the whole truth, and nothing but the truth?''

She grinned like a mean little kid as they disengaged, and then she told him, ''I didn't want them hurting that other girl. The name she gave me was Valya Sikorski and she might have been Russian. I never asked, but she talked funny. She was the one I told you about. The one I felt so sorry for when we met on the walk the night of that robbery. If I say so myself, I'd fitted her out with much nicer clothes just a few months before. So I knew she was in some sort of fix, before those men barged in to ask me where she'd gone!''

Longarm suggested they go back inside her dress shop, explaining, ''This landing's likely to be crowded in a few minutes, and this time you get to attend the inquest too. From what I heard through your door, no offense, it wasn't too clear to me whether they were looking for this Russian Val who used to work at Madame Velvet's, or whether they were trying to find out whether you'd recognized her the night of the robbery as one of your customers.''

Leading the way inside, Elvira asked, ''How could they have known where Russian Val got her dresses here in Mulligan? Who could have told them if they don't know where she is right now?''

Longarm smiled thinly and explained, ''You might have got the whole line of questioning backwards, through no fault of your own trusting nature. If this Russian Val was scouting for the gang the night of the robbery, they've known all along where she's been hiding out with them. So what if they were trying to find out how much *you* knew, and how much you'd told *me,* about a gal we both might have heard them mention as their boss? They did say they were taking you to a boss lady, remember?''

The honest dressmaking widow gasped, ''A woman, that *kind* of woman, leading a gang of outlaws?''

To which Longarm replied with a shrug, "Why not? she'd know this neck of the woods better than outlaws drifting in, or summoned, from other parts. And outlaws by definition don't play by the usual rules of any gentleman's code. And a local mastermind might eliminate a whole peck of puzzles around here."

Chapter 12

Elvira Tenkiller kept simple business records in pencil in a loose-leaf notebook. So they'd soon estabished that she'd last sewn a ripped seam for one Valya Sikorski of 27 Mine Road about the time of Madame Velvet's death, close to two weeks before the robbery.

Longarm took down the names of other customers residing in a house of ill repute, noting none had been back since before their madam had died. He suggested, and Elvira agreed, it looked as if the failing health of both Madame Velvet and the town of Mulligan had inspired a stampede for greener pastures. Durango and other new settlements over on the west slope in recent Indian lands were more poorly supplied with ring-dang-doo than young single gents drawing boomtown pocket jingle. Longarm had just suggested the mysterious Russian Val might have stayed on in Mulligan with someone who didn't cotton to regular wages, when Undersheriff Babcock came in to join them without knocking.

Babcock ticked his hat brim to Elvira and told Longarm, "You're a real barrel of monkeys, and who needs an opera house when *you're* here to entertain us with two shoot-outs in less than twenty-four hours?"

Longarm smiled modestly and replied, "I do my best to please. What time is the inquest?"

The older lawman replied, "Doc Maytag ain't decided. He has a drugstore to run, you know. I sent your latest playmate yonder to cool off in the cellar. What was that about there being one to go again?"

Longarm shrugged and said, "They keep sending them out in pairs. I figure there were at least four men and a woman to begin with. Two down makes it three to go."

Elvira said, "They were trying to kidnap me. One made mention of a feminine mastermind just before Custis, thank God, came out of nowhere to my rescue!"

The undersheriff shot Longarm a puzzled look and asked, "Then they weren't after *you* this time?"

Longarm said, "They were after Miss Elvira here to tell them how much I knew about that mousy gal they sent in ahead to scout the post office for them that night. Had they stayed hidden, it might have taken us a lot longer to learn we're looking for a fallen woman named Valya Sikorski, better known as Russian Val. She speaks with a furrin accent, likely Slavic. Miss Elvira here would be better than me at describing her."

The older lawman got out his own notebook as the dressmaker who'd measured Russian Val for more than one fitting said, "She'd be somewhere in her mid-to-late thirties, give or take the line of work she's in. She has brown eyes and naturally brown hair, rinsed with henna on some occasions and possibly plain old dirt on others. She has a round face with regular features that can be painted up pretty or toned down drab with a dust rag. She stands about five foot two, and would weigh about a hundred and twenty-five or thirty. Just under what you men call pleasingly plump, and I suppose you'd say she had a spectacular hourglass shape with her corset on. She's just a bit dumpy without it."

Undersheriff Babcock looked away as he softly remarked, "I've heard talk in the Chloride Saloon about one of Madame Velvet's gals who had a funny way of talking and some unusual ways of . . . entertaining. I have my senior deputies out canvassing for a line on which way that one on horseback might have headed. With four likely escape routes, and dozens more for a desperado cutting cross-country over open range, I figured we ought to have an educated guess as to which way we're riding before we posse up!''

Longarm asked if Babcock had wired north to Golden and east to Denver. The older lawman snorted in disgust and asked, ''Why don't you go teach your granny to churn butter? I telegraphed Idaho Springs whilst I was over to the Western Union. There's a chance he'd aim for tall timber on the higher slopes to the west.''

Longarm had been thinking before he decided aloud, ''He won't light out across open range. The bunch of them have been holed up all the time in or about Mulligan. I have a list of company cabins, rented or up for rent, and there are other buildings public and private here in town. There's a chance they've holed up at a homestead or stock spread a short lope off in any direction. But that one who ran for it just now would have run home first to Mother, and I just can't see two men and a woman breaking cover to light out across open range in broad daylight. I suspect a hideout, and a clever one, was the inspiration for that post office robbery to begin with.''

Neither the dressmaker nor the older lawman seemed to follow Longarm's drift. So he asked, ''Shall we count the ways you rob a post office in a small town at twilight? You get in and get out with the cash to vanish in the tricky light of the gloaming. Then you have two main choices. You can ride hell-for-leather through the night and hope to be long gone by the time the posse can cut your trail by the dawn's first light. Or you can shuck your disguises and simply go home, if you have a home to go to that close to the scene of the crime. Four men and a woman or more could easily fit inside a miner's cabin or a single hotel room if they kept the noise down and nobody hung out the windows waving at the posse forming up."

Babcock nodded grudgingly, but asked, "Let's say that explains why we never cut any trail in the first light of dawn after the robbery. Where in the U.S. Constitution does it say they had to stay here in town all this time? They've had more than enough time to just split up and drift on—or for that matter leave in a bunch?"

Longarm said, "They could of. But they didn't. If they had, neither the two yesterday nor the two today would be showing so much interest in this child. That's the one sign I've cut that they never should have left me. Like you said, they could have just left town a long time before I got here. Had they felt too sentimental about Mulligan to leave, they'd have still been better off leaving me to flounder all about with nothing to tell me they were anywhere in Colorado at this late date. I've never laid eyes on this Russian Val, and she seems to be able to change her appearance at will in any case. I never saw the late Pecos Tim Sheehan before he made me shoot him yesterday. I still don't know who that was I just shot on the landing outside, and that other one who owes his life to Miss Elvira kicking him in the shins was a stranger to me too. That leaves one male member of the gang I may or may not know on sight, assuming there's only the four we know of for sure."

Babcock pointed out, "Strangers hiding out here in town without a paid-up resident reporting it would have to be in cahoots with a paid-up resident, making it *more* than the four who pulled that one robbery, right?"

Longarm shook his head and said, "My elimination boss says it's best to stick with numbers you know for sure. Say a local boy screwed one of Madame Velvet's out-of-work hookers. Sorry, ma'am, there's no nicer way to put it. Say he recruited only *three* owlhoot riders to join him in a job he'd planned for some time but couldn't pull off alone. I suspect the nearby *hideout* was a greater temptation than the modest contents of a small-town post office safe. Mention of a female mastermind might mean an out-of-work hooker who'd already used the post office to send money orders back East or even to Russia could have put the job together, scouted for her lover and three pals, and had the coffee on by the time they made their getaway on foot in the cool shade of evening.''

Babcock shrugged and said, "Gals do seem to get more attached to a place. But we know they have at least two ponies at their disposal, and you ain't the first or only lawman hunting them serious for that federal offense against the post office. And they seem mighty worried about you and you in particular hunting for them in these parts. So what in tarnation are they *doing* in these parts? I mean, they could have lit out the moment they heard you might be coming, before you got here!''

The pretty dressmaker had been trying to follow their talk, but had to cut in with: "How can anyone be certain they were expecting Custis here in particular?''

The two lawmen exchanged glances. When he saw Babcock was leaving it to him to say something, Longarm said, "They were laying for me in ambush long before I could get here. They were just now asking you what I knew about Russian Val. You were there when they mentioned me by name.''

She sighed and said, "I was, and I'm still at a loss for a proper way to repay you for saving me from who knows what fate. But what does it all mean, Custis? I'm only a girl, but I can see it would make more sense for the bunch of them to just leave you alone and go somewhere else!''

Longarm pursed his lips thoughtfully and tried, "At least one of 'em may have no better place to go. Say the one I've yet to lay eyes on could be someone I'd recognize at a distance the moment I laid eyes on him. Say he's some notorious outlaw most *any* lawman might recognize on sight. Then say that while riding the owlhoot trail through less settled high country, he met up with Russian Val as she was moving out or getting thrown out of Madame Velvet's place. Say they screwed—there's no nicer way to put it—with him avoiding the light of day as Russian Val did the shopping, cased all the cash tills along Main Street as their original funds ran low, and then let's say he spied three drifters he knew from other parts drifting through on their way to elsewhere.''

Undersheriff Babcock said, ''I like it. A gal who knows the town masterminding the job. Her lover boy somebody famous as Jesse or The Kid holed up with her right here in town, nipping out now and again just long enough to rob up a post office, ambush a lawman, or try and kidnap a local businesswoman, but afraid to ride far in public lest somebody recognize him for certain and even spot his gal before they could get out of Jefferson County. From what they were saying about Russian Val in the Chloride Saloon, riders came in from far and wide for her . . . services.''

''What perversion was she famous for?'' Elvira asked in womanly interest.

The older lawman actually blushed and murmured, ''There's some things a gentleman don't mention in front of his own wife, ma'am. Suffice to say, Russian Val seems mighty well known in her own right. And any woman riding across open range with one or more male riders is likely to be remembered at any spreads they'd whipped on by acting stuck-up.''

Longarm told the dressmaker, ''What he means is that riders out this way are expected to stop for water and directions when they get within hailing distance of any human habitation. The lady of the house or hired cook may or may not invite 'em in for coffee and cake as well. But whether they do or they don't, they're apt to feel insulted by passing strangers who don't give them any chance to *ask*. So even owlhoot riders pass a place acting snooty at their peril, and like my pard here suggests, a famous outlaw screwing a famous fallen woman might be more scared of breaking cover than he is of me uncovering him.''

Babcock speculated on whether Jesse James or Billy the

Kid could be hiding out under their noses in Mulligan. Longarm pointed out that the James boys had been spotted recently in Missouri, while some said The Kid had been seen washing dishes for his grub along the border. ''I like somebody more distinctive at a distance and wanted federal. And we have a tedious list of unusually tall, short, thick, thin, or crippled-up owlhoot riders we'd like to arrest. It ain't wise for a hunter to picture his game before he spots it. Sometimes a man with his heart set on pheasant can stare right through a plump quail. So all I know is that there's at least two men and a gal out there in the middle distance, hoping I don't see them first.''

The older lawman said he had to get back down and see how his own bunch was making out. Longarm said he'd be along directly, and stayed when Babcock left.

As soon as they were alone, Longarm took out his own hotel key and handed it to Elvira. He said, ''You'd best lock up and leave first. I'll cover you from discreet pistol range whilst you go up the slope and circle back to the Drover's Rest. You know where it is, don't you?''

She stared down dubiously at the key in her hand as she replied in a strained voice, ''Of course I do. I live here in Mulligan, but, ah . . . Custis, when I said I was anxious to repay you for saving my life I didn't have . . . *that* in mind.''

He laughed incredulously and said, ''I used to think it was us boys who had dirty minds. I ain't out to have my wicked way with you in my hotel room, no offense. I just want to make sure nobody tries to kidnap you again before I can figure a better way to guard your body and soul. I ain't going back to my hotel directly. I want you to slip in the rear entrance from the stable out back, mosey upstairs without mentioning it to anyone, and let yourself into the room that goes with the number on that tag. There's a pitcher of water and two tumblers on the bureau, and you'll find a fifth of Maryland rye in one of my saddlebags, along with back issues of the *Police Gazette* and a more recent issue of *Leslie's Magazine*. If you get hungry, I got some canned beans and tomato preserves in the bedroll lashed to the same saddle. Here, you'd best hang on to this pocket-knife for me. It has a a can-opening blade.''

As he handed her his pocketknife he added, ''I'll likely be back before supper time, though. By then I'll know when Doc Maytag will want us to attend another inquest. He's sure to want us both as eyewitnesses. So you'll have a socially acceptable excuse to have a sit-down supper with me, and by then I may have figured out a more seemly hideout for you.''

She almost wailed, ''But why do I have to hide out at all? I haven't done anything to anybody!''

He said soothingly, ''You know that and I know that, Miss Elvira. But they just now came here to your fitting room to pester you. So the odds are they know where your company cabin is and . . . You do live alone, don't you?''

She sniffed and said, ''I told you my husband was killed in the mine. What kind of a woman do you think I am?''

He said, ''I would have been mortally surprised if you'd told me you were living with an outlaw, ma'am. We'll talk about it some more this evening. But right now we'd best get cracking.''

She protested, ''Why can't I just tag along with you until this evening then? Where are you going that I can't come along with you?''

Longarm hesistated, then shook his head and told her, ''Way too complicated, ma'am. Once I make sure you're safe from the other side, I'll be on my way to that house of ill repute where Russian Val was reputed to behave so wicked.''

Elvira blinked and protested, ''But Custis, Valya Sikor-ski doesn't work there anymore!''

Longarm nodded, but said, ''She used to, and I got to start somewhere if I hope to cut her trail.''

Chapter 13

Longarm found Cordelia Gilliam out back in the whore-house garden, down on her knees in a denim smock with old Gus, the man-of-all-work they'd brought from Kansas. They were pulling weeds. It was just as well. Because when she shot Longarm an arch look over one shoulder, it was as if she didn't have that faded blue denim over her shapely rump and Longarm was fixing to go at her dog-style again.

But she stayed calm as still waters while old Gus said modesty forbade him to take the credit for such a swell garden that far out of the ground in a Rocky Mountain Maytime. Gus explained most of the perennials had been there under a tidy straw mulch when he'd come out west with the new owners and simply raked it away and let the already greening-up vegetation grab for the morning suns of spring. He said all those carrots, peas, runner beans, and such they were clearing of late spring weeds had been started in a planting tray over yonder in a lean-to green-house Longarm could see against the south wall of the carriage house. Longarm resisted the impulse to hunker down and grab hold of that one sassy plantain sticking its little green tongue out at him, and asked Cordelia if she knew where Lawyer Portia might be.

Cordelia said Portia was inside with her big sister, going

over an offer for the property from the short-line stagecoach company. So he went inside to find them in the kitchen with the older man's motherly housekeeping wife. They naturally invited him to sit down for some coffee and cake at the same table. So he did.

He let them explain the typed-up contract offer they had spread out on the table between them. Longarm had already noticed that the Drover's Rest charged regular hotel rates for bad accommodations with no running water, and that the recent nice weather was all that stood between a guest there and the extremes of summer and winter in the treeless foothills of the Front Range. Portia said the coach line wanted to buy a well-built good-sized building with indoor plumbing and steam heat as a worthy rival of the Drover's Rest. The sticking point was that the company based in Golden insisted—and it was hard to argue with them—that Mulligan's days were numbered, their spur line was unlikely to last past the coming turn of the century, and so they didn't want to pay the going price for sturdy frame mansions in the Denver area.

Portia's advice was to take such money as they could still get in a one-business town depending on one mine having drainage problems. Longarm had already gotten the impression that the older sister and namesake of Madame Velvet was either a tad piggish or, like all too many spinster gals, afraid of getting screwed, literally or figuratively.

As Longarm was served, Cyn said she'd read back in Wichita how empty lots sold for better than two hundred dollars a square foot and rents started at three hundred a month for stores and ten dollars a week for unfurnished flats.

Longarm gently told her, "Two hundred a *front foot* or the width of the lot facing the street, ma'am. And those rents are gold-rush rents. Not dying-on-the-vine rents. To compete with the Drover's Rest, the coach line couldn't charge much more than an extra two bits a night in wintertime when steam heat matters. So I'd say Miss Portia here could advise you better than a Kansas newspaper on the Colorado real-estate market.''

He sipped more coffee to be polite, and added, ''I have to attend a coroner's hearing this evening. What I'm here for this afternoon is to look at Madame Velvet's later entries in her drawn-out diary. Before I do, might either of you recall the name of Valya Sikorski, better known as Russian Val?''

The two American women exchanged blank looks. Longarm explained his suspicions about one of Madame Velvet's soiled doves staying on in Mulligan after quitting, being fired, or being paid off there at the recent house of ill repute.

Portia said, ''I naturally made everyone my clients bought out sign a quit-claim. So while that name doesn't ring any bells, I have carbons in my files if you'd like to come upstairs with me.''

That sounded like a swell notion to Longarm, but when he kicked the door of her room shut behind them way upstairs, Portia never gave him the chance to grab an old pal where he wanted to grab her. She laughed lightly and said, ''Down, boy! It's barely past noon and we are not alone in this whorehouse! How would it look to my clients if their lawyer screwed in the afternoon?''

Longarm wistfully replied, ''Like they had a friendly lawyer? I can take a hint. Tell me how much they paid Russian Val to get her off the premises to somewhere too close for comfort.''

Portia said they'd already heard about his more recent shoot-out up Main Street as she hauled out her files. As she went through them on the bed, she asked if he wanted her to represent him at the inquest.

He said, ''Thanks just the same, but they'll likely be holding it in the Chloride Saloon and I've been through the tedious questioning in the past. It was open-and-shut in front of a respectable local witness. I'm more worried about who the rascals were working for. I doubt she'd have told you to call her Russian Val. Valya Sikorski would be more like it.''

Portia replied, ''I'm looking, I'm looking, but I don't see any Sikorski by any first name here, and the sisters only had to buy out half a dozen gals. See for yourself. Most of the poor drabs had seen the handwriting on the wall before my clients arrived a little over a week ago.''

Longarm took the list she'd made on a separate sheet of notepaper before drawing up the quit-claims. He recognized two of the names as customers Elvira Tenkiller had shown him. The others meant nothing to him, and there was no name as outlandish as Sikorski or even Schultz.

Handing the list back, Longarm decided, ''Reckon I just can't get out of hunting her up in the diary of Madame Velvet then. Russian Val ought to appear in that last volume, seeing she was here around the time the old bawd died and seeing the old bawd wrote down all the naughty bits. The word around town is that Russian Val went in for downright nasty bits, and the Madame seems to have wanted to record such history for all time. You'd think she'd have wanted to brag on her swell garden.''

Portia didn't offer to go back up to the old woman's room with him. Alone with the nineteen spicy volumes and the feather bed he'd shared with sassy little Cordelia, Longarm sat down at that writing table to backtrack Russian Val.

The poor old whore's unfinished last entry wisfully recorded how tough she was finding it to breathe the thin mountain air all about, how little those pills from Doc Maytag really helped the lonely chest pains late at night, and how she was really dying for a nice lusty roll in the feathers with a well-hung hardworking man who didn't need a bath too bad.

There was nothing about Russian Val, even though the Madame herself had been a tad shocked by a request the current mine supervisor had made involving French Lily and a guard dog he was mighty fond of.

Other entries were as graphic. Madame Velvet hadn't

seemed to be holding anything back as she recorded who'd done what to whom, for how much, downstairs.

He set that volume aside and tried an earlier one, with the same mysterious results. He heard the door open behind him, and assuming it was Portia said, "I can only make this work two possible ways. A wild and wicked local hooker was only telling the boys in town that she worked here, or before she left, Russian Val or some other wicked soul doctored these books!"

"What makes you think that?" asked a voice that didn't go with his pal Portia Parkhurst as soft female hands crept over his shoulders and down his chest.

When a heroic set of tits shoved his hat off to land upside down across the pages he'd been scanning, Longarm said, "Afternoon, Miss Cyn. I was just telling your lawyer we got us a problem here. You and your sister never paid her off, and it appears at first glance Madame Velvet never met her either. So there's either a mysterious imposter taking advantage of the changes here to make up a past she never had, or she *had* a past here and covered it up by fiddling at these diary entries and—what are you doing down yonder, Miss Cyn?"

She purred, "Trying to unbuckle this clumsy gun belt, you silly. Why would anyone want to forge my aunt's naughty diary, and don't try to tell me you and our lawyer weren't being naughty up here last night. I heard you when I came up the stairs with some hot chocolate to share with you. I could tell the two of you didn't want to be disturbed."

Longarm was damned if he said it had been Portia, and damned if he said it hadn't been. So he said, "I can't see any way to erase ink on this brand of coated stationary. It's the same kind of paper they use on bank checks and legal documents. You ain't *supposed* to be able to change facts and figures once they've been set down to keep and cherish. The only way you could delete each and every passage about a certain name appearing in these volumes would be to start over from scratch on blank diary pages with the same sort of ink in the same handwriting and just add or subtract any words you needed to, see?''

He grabbed his holster to keep his .44-40 from falling to the rug as she finished unbuckling his gun rig and demanded in a cooing tone, ''Who but Aunt Cyn could have done this, and why? Aren't all those old confessions about more important people written in the same hand? I don't see how this mysterious Russian girl could have copied at least one whole volume from scratch in the little time she'd have had to work with, even if she'd been a master forger and had a sensible motive to alter even one volume!''

As she tried to slide one hand down the front of Longarm's pants with her soft cheek against his, her soft breasts pressed against his back and her perfume sure to stink up his tweeds for that inquest later on, Longarm sighed and said, ''When you're right you're right. I only see two ways to forge and alter handwritten text from scratch. You'd have to be one thundering wonder of a forger, capable of faking a distinctive handwriting to where your one new volume matched eighteen other samples to the T. Or you'd have to rewrite the whole dad-blamed shebang from scratch, all nineteen volumes!''

Cyn nibbled his ear, crooning, ''That's impossible, and wouldn't we be more comfortable over on the bed if you must go on and on about a dirty old lady's mental masturbation!''

He stayed put with his hand gripping her wrist gently but firmly as he said, ''I'd be proud to take you up on such an offer some other time, Miss Cyn. I've always suspected Casanova was sort of jerking off with his pen, and he went on and on about how much the gals all liked him. But this is important. A whole saloon full of satisfied customers testify to a wild and wanton Russian Val working here around the time your late aunt died. Yet your late aunt never mentions her name, and we know she wrote down scandalous things about some of the most important men who ever strode the stage of Colorado history in past and recent booms and busts. So how come you say it's impossible that Russian Val simply rewrote her own part in Colorado history? If she was here in the building when the old lady was found dead on this very floor, she might have had the opportunity to rewrite all nineteen volumes in her own hand! Nobody photographed the originals, did they?''

Cyn moved around to sit in his lap and rub against him like a cat that was being ignored by a houseguest as she insisted, ''It's obvious. Ask Portia. There wasn't *time*. Her firm was on retainer to the fallen but far-from-broke black sheep of the family. Portia advised us of our rights under Colorado laws, and we folded up our tents in Wichita and got right out here. All these volumes of handwriting you see up here in her room would have taken months, not weeks, to transcribe from the beginning—where in volume one Aunt Cyn allowed she'd become a fallen woman but didn't feel like killing herself, and wasn't even ashamed. Say nobody asked this mysterious Russian Val what she was doing up in this room. It would have taken her the better part of a week to fake one volume, writing naturally and getting questioned by everyone else on the premises!''

Longarm decided, ''It's possible but mighty impractical as soon as you toss in possible motives. A body capable of writing fairly close to the style others might have on hand in the form of letters home and such would find it *possible* to recopy three hundred-odd entries to a volume in, say, a month of gut-busting homework, cribbing from the real entries to save having to stop and think, whilst editing out the parts that mentioned one gal, in possibly two or three of the last volumes. But to what end? If Russian Val didn't want her name to appear in the diary of Madame Velvet, it would have been easier for her to just get rid of it all. Were you even expecting to find such complete records of a long eventful life, Miss Cyn?''

She moved over to flop petulantly in the bed in her thin cotton shift as Longarm rebuckled his gun rig. She pouted.

''Pooh, you're no fun! But to answer your question, I might never have considered some of the things I've been considering lately if I hadn't read every volume from cover to cover. You're so right about her having led an eventful life. Maybe there just wasn't room for that other wild and wicked wanton in her last volume or so. They barely give you one page for each evening's scribble-scrabble, and another thing, where would a suddenly reformed whore get twenty-four volumes to scribble-scrabble in a town this size?''

Longarm frowned and replied, ''Twenty-four, Miss Cyn? I make it nineteen volumes she wrote in, counting this last one with more than half its pages still blank.''

The spinster gal he'd mistaken for the shy one shook her head and told him, ''Twenty-four. Five of them on a shelf in the hall closet, never used. It looks as if she bought blank diaries by the dozen in the days of yore. If she filled up the first dozen, then bought a second dozen, how long back, seven years ago . . . ?''

Longarm rose from the table as he replied, ''The figures add that way for me. Before I chase my tail around the same tree again, I'd better find out whether it was possible for Russian Val to buy that same brand of stationery-store diary. They ought to be able to tell me at the one stationery store in town. That's what my boss calls eliminating. You find out if something *could* have been done before you accuse anybody of *doing* it.''

Chapter 14

Those never-used volumes in the hall closet eliminated questions, raised other questions, and saved a fuss with the forward and willful Cynthia Gilliam, who said she'd never allow any of Madame Velvet's bodacious confessions out of her possession for nothing.

She agreed to let Longarm traipse over to the one stationery store in town with 366 blank pages bound in goatskin embossed to look like alligator.

That little old lady who ran the shop under Elvira's dressmaking business made him tell her what all that shooting had been about a while ago, and once he had, told him they didn't carry that line of blank diaries. She said she suspected by the maker's mark that they were sold through mail order, and rustled up some mail-order catalogues to make certain. As she was pawing through them, Longarm decided he could use a new pocket notebook, seeing the one he had on him was halfway filled and she was being such a good sport.

She proved it by placing a mail-order catalogue and a daily diary from her own stock side by side on the counter, saying, "I thought I remembered that sample you brought in from another customer's request for a blank match for a shoddier brand. This diary we sell for fifty cents is a better buy by far. We don't handle stock made up from sham alligator and wood-pulp paper coated to resemble linen bond. It wouldn't pay to haul it by freight wagon from Denver even if we weren't calling ourselves a *stationery* shop!''

Longarm said he understood, not certain he did, and asked if she thought it likely a lady economizing on her paper goods might ask for them to sell her ''baker's dozens'' by mail.

She shook her head and replied, ''Not according to the already low terms they offer here in print. These shoddy diaries with delusions of glory *are* cheaper by the dozen. But they send you a dozen for the price of eleven. Is that a clue?''

He smiled thinly and replied with a nod, ''It's another elimination, ma'am. Two extra volumes missing from a set might have explained some hows, if not some whys. I can't see anyone who's moved around as far and wide as . . . the lady who was keeping this brand of blank diaries, would have bought two dozen to begin with and lugged them all over the mining country for nigh twenty years. I suspect she'd have bought one a year, over the years, like that customer you just mentioned. You, ah, wouldn't care to tell me who that other diary keeper might be, I suppose?''

She sniffed and said, ''You suppose right. But to set your mind at ease, she's a respectable married woman, and I've never sold anything but some stationery and envelopes to any of those painted women over at Madam Velvet's.''

He chuckled fondly and said, ''I'm sorry if I shocked you when I told you as much as I had to about my quest for stationery sources, ma'am. But you've proved me right by answering some questions smart and helpful. I got one more. Seeing it's hardly likely anyone would tote a twenty-four-year supply of blank diary volumes over hill and dale before they were needed, ain't there no place out here in Colorado a body could buy that brand of shoddy merchandise a volume at a time retail in, say, a neighborhood notions store?''

The old woman, who prided herself on quality wares, shrugged and said, ''I can hardly speak for every pushcart peddler west of the wide Missouri, young sir. But isn't it likely Madame Velvet simply sent for a new blank volume once a year, as she filled them up?''

Longarm thought, then decided, ''Let's split the difference and say she was too refined to buy things cheaper by the dozen. Does that there catalogue offer her chosen brand one at a time?''

The old lady looked, shook her gray head, and said, ''Four for a dollar. A dozen for two-fifty. That's too much for wood-pulp bond, if you ask me!''

He hadn't asked what she thought of the confessions of Madame Velvet. She hadn't read them, and he for one had no intention of showing them to any respectable woman.

He thanked her, put his new notebook in a side pocket, and ambled on to the post office, reflecting that it was a good thing Mulligan's business district only extended a little over a city block each way from the intersection of Main Street and Mine Road. For at the rate he was going, he was sure defining the term ''legwork'' as all too many lawmen knew it to their chagrin.

It couldn't be helped. A dog who didn't want to sniff never caught many rabbits. At the post office Longarm found old Ash Woodside and a younger gent in a gartered-sleeve white shirt but denim jeans at work behind the counter with cancellation stamps.

Longarm knew what they were doing. But the postmaster still told him they were postmarking the outgoing mail bound for Golden by way of that short line's morning stagecoach to Golden. Ash introduced his younger sidekick as Fred Waller, and said he was that assistant they'd talked about who handled special delivery. When asked, Waller modestly allowed he rode mail sacks directly into Denver whenever they'd sold enough special-delivery stamps. Otherwise the mail rode by coach to Golden to be sorted and sent on one way or the other from the bigger post office at the county seat.

Longarm asked, in that case, whether money orders as well as parcel post from mail-order houses were likely to come down from Golden aboard the same coaches. It was young Waller who told him that was about the size of it, and added, "We've talked about that. Those outlaws who hit us around Mayday could have stopped the coach outside of town with all those end-of-the-month money orders, but they'd have only wound up with the money orders. Ash, here, had the *cash* on hand to redeem them!"

Ash Woodside explained, "Armored post office wagon. Comes down a few days early with an armed escort. The outlaws doubtless figured I was a tad easier to get by working alone here. They even waited until Fred was out making a delivery before they hit!"

Fred Waller said, "One of the mine company dicks was saying you'd figured that gal they sent in ahead to scout for them was one of Madame Velvet's whores?"

Longarm nodded and said, "I was getting to that. I came here to ask you gents about mail-order deliveries to Madame Velvet's place since just after she died last month."

The two post office men exchanged glances. Ash Woodside decided, "I wasn't invited to the funeral, but didn't that old bawd die of a heart stroke in the middle of April, say ten or fifteen days before the robbery?"

Fred Waller said, "You don't have to look it up, Ash. I'm the one who'd have toted the load, and I never did. Not any time in April, and for certain not after she *died*! Madame Velvet didn't allow her whores to give her street address as their own. They had to send and receive such mail as whores ever send or receive right here at this counter. I don't know what made Madame Velvet so stuck up about that."

Longarm said, "I do. If you allow a whore to give your address as your own, you may have some explaining to do when, not if, she's picked up by the law on one charge or another.''

A sudden thought hit him. He laughed and asked, ''Do you remember when you were a kid, how you'd be laying in bed at night and all of a sudden you'd be seeing critters or spooky faces in the shadows all about your bed? I think that last question may have just answered a mystery that was no mystery at all!''

Ash Woodside demanded he do better than that. So Longarm explained, ''I've been gnawing on some names left out of an old whore's brags like a hound sniffing for bones where no bones may be buried! That Russian Val who took it three ways for one dollar stands convicted by her own sneaky actions as a sneaky no-good gal, willing to combine her crimes against nature with interfering with the U.S. mails. So what if Madame Velvet, only known to us as a dedicated whore, let Russian Val go, after a short trial period, and never wrote nothing about what a disgusting time she'd had with her because she *knew,* as a wise old pussy peddler, that Russian Val would surely wind up on Uncle Sam's shit list?''

Longarm realized he was speculating aloud when neither of them were able to follow his drift. He said, ''I was talking about the diary of Madame Velvet. You'd have to read it. At the rate things are going, you well may do so. But the literary estate of Madame Velvet ain't our problem, praise the Lord.''

He thanked them, and they all shook and parted friendly. Longarm went next to the nearby Drover's Rest, and slipped upstairs to rap on his locked door, identify himself to Elvira Tenkiller, and sneak in to find her distraught and pacing, with some of that Maryland rye he'd told her about on her breath as she gasped, ''Where have you been all this time? I've been going crazy all alone up here! It only came to me after you'd left that you'd told me Russian Val, or some other low woman, had been asking about you down at the desk!''

112

Longarm set the blank diary volume aside for safekeeping as he told her, "I knew that. I wouldn't have been able to tell you if I hadn't known that. The other side has to know I'm here in Mulligan, and this is the only hotel I could have gone to. They sent that gal last night to see where *else* in town I might be prowling. They ain't worried about me catching any of them here at this hotel. They're worried about me finding out where *they* have been *staying*.

"I just came from the post office. I may have just made some pieces of the puzzle fit a tad more sensible. To begin with, I suspect Russian Val didn't spend much time at Madame Velvet's. I suspect she'd found her own quarters here in Mulligan, where she was serving a select clientele of one. A famous outlaw Madame Velvet recognized offers one easy answer to more than one question. You don't want one of your gals entertaining a serious outlaw on the premises.

"So let's say Russian Val was the sole play-pretty of somebody mean, even before you did some fashionable sewing for her. Let's say with the end of the month coming on and the small post office of a mining town ripe for the plucking, they recruited those other guns. Let's say that later, after they'd pulled it off and were just laying low to let their trail cool, they learned I'd been assigned to the case. I'm still working on why I scared 'em that much. But then let's say they were watching me at a safe distance, noticed I'd been talking to you, were worried you knew something, and here we are."

She sniffed, "Here we are indeed! That dumpy Russian girl I fitted for more modest street clothes is the *leader* of the pack! You were there, just outside the door, when the one you killed said they were taking me to *her* and letting *her* decide!"

Longarm had been wondering where she'd put his Maryland rye. She tottered over to the washstand in the corner to refill her hotel tumbler as she added, "Custis, I'm scared! I've been pacing and pacing, trying to figure out why they

113

came after little old me when they knew all the time where you were!''

Longarm modestly replied, ''Mayhaps they didn't expect you to pack a six-gun. They didn't do too well when they tried to ambush me alone on the open range. Gunning anyone in the middle of a town attracts some attention. They weren't fixing to gun you, and you're a gal, if they didn't have to. That fight on the stairs wasn't what they'd come to you for. I doubt the survivors were at all pleased with the results. They'd be out of their heads to come after a man who's whupped them twice, especially in his own hotel, forted up behind a locked door with two guns they know of for certain and a derringer they ought to at least suspect me capable of.''

She looked uncertain. He insisted, ''They have no way of knowing you're up here as a prize more worth the fight. Even if they did and even if they were mad with desire for you, they'd wind up in a dreadful fix if they *won*!''

He took off his hat and coat, but left his .44-40 on while he explained. ''They robbed the post office at twilight so's to vanish in tricky light to a nearby hidey-hole. That was before any of us were *looking* for said hidey-hole. Everyone's first natural notion was that they'd ridden out across the open range. The James-Younger gang might have escaped unscathed had they ducked into a hidey-hole right in Northfield instead of riding off in a hail of bullets that time. The one who got away today at your dress shop wasn't *expecting* to have to run for it. He was *forced* to, and so far he seems to have been lucky. But Undersheriff Babcock has his own men out canvassing for him and that other pony. They'll be backtracking the town livery and the very stable of this hotel for the cow pony we captured in front of your place. So even if I say so myself, you're as safe here as any other address I can come up with here in Mulligan, unless you'd care to spend the night with me in jail.''

Elvira gulped, refilled her tumbler, and asked with an

114

uncertain smile, ''Were we fixing to spend the night to-gether anywhere?''

He shrugged and said, ''I doubt if it'll come to forting up in the jail for the night, Miss Elvira. I thought of taking you over to this other place I know. But in truth the down-stairs there ain't watched around the clock by desk clerks, and you might feel awkward spending the night in a not-quite-empty house of ill repute. So all in all, I figure this is about our best bet. Having lost two of their gun hands messing with this child in broad day, I doubt the ones left will risk an assault on this hotel when, for all they know, I could be laying for them in another room.''

Elvira shrugged in resignation, drained her glass, and heaved a great sigh as she calmly began to unbutton her bodice, smiling sort of like Miss Mona Lisa as she observed half to herself, ''Oh, well, you've been out of mourning for more than a year and it's not as if poor Gene wouldn't understand.''

Longarm started to say he'd been planning on letting her have the bed while he spread the bedroll from his saddle on the rug. But then, as the petite brunette proceeded to shuck her summer frock and get into bed in her sateen shimmy shirt, he wondered why any man would ever want to say something as stupid as that.

Chapter 15

Thanks to its earlier teasing at the hands of Cyn Gilliam, his old organ-grinder would have risen to the occasion even if Elvira hadn't flashed such shapely legs climbing into bed in her shimmy shirt in the dappled sunlight scattered across the bedding by window curtains of cotton crochet. But Longarm was hard as a rock by the time he had it in her, after trying in vain to get her out of that shimmy shirt so a man could see what he was getting into.

It sure felt swell, whatever it looked like, and she proved she'd been happily married a spell back by wrapping those sun-spangled tawny legs around him and biting down hard, at both ends, as she liked to swallowed his poor tongue.

He got her out of that cotton sateen chemise once he'd made her come and she'd gotten over her first shock. She confessed with burning cheeks that she'd never expected him to get in bed *naked* with her, and he believed her when she said it made her feel depraved to go bare-ass belly-to-belly with him, although she seemed to like it a lot.

He'd found in his travels that gals raised at opposite ends of the Victorian pecking order were willing to get into bed stark naked. The poor white trash were willing to strip down completely. The more artistic and well-to-do white folks also felt more comfortable going at it in their birthday

116

suits. Middle-class to working-poor white or colored folks were told it was wrong to fuck stark naked by day or lamplight. They were supposed to wear nightgowns or at least some underwear, and make sure it was pitch dark before they went that far.

Longarm had never figured out who told them this. They'd never told *him*, or some West-by-God-Virginia trash he'd always remember fondly. But he thought it best to assure the Cherokee breed he was undressing with his shaft still in her that he knew young ladies of quality down Texas way and back East on that Long Island who even blew the French horn stark naked with the bedroom lamps lit.

She told him not to even think of her committing crimes against nature in total darkness, but added, with a teasing thrust of her hips, "It does feel lovely with your hairy chest against my bare . . . breasts, and since we really shouldn't be doing this at all, I guess there's no sense worrying you'll remember me as a halfbreed whore!"

Longarm placed a firm but gentle palm on her tailbone to get it in deeper as he gently replied, "I don't recall you asking me for a dime, Miss Elvira. A whore by definition is a woman who fucks men for money."

She began to move faster and hug him back as she sobbed, "What do you call this if it's not . . . fucking?"

She blushed dusky rose and marveled, "My God! I said that word! I have a man's dirty *thing* up inside me and I just admitted what we were doing right out loud!"

He kissed her and got her even hotter as he insisted, "You're not fucking a customer for money, Miss Elvira. You're fucking a friend for pleasure. You do find this pleasing, I hope?"

She moaned, "Oh, Christ, yessss! I've never felt this hot and dirty and it pleases the hell out of me! My God, what's come over me? I'm not supposed to say hell either. But I don't care! I just want to fuck like hell just for the hell of it, with no sweet nothings about forever while you make

117

me come, because forever is a lie and all I want from you or any man is a good hot come from head to toes!''

So Longarm spread her legs wider with an elbow hooked under either knee, and ignored her protests that he was splitting her like a fucking wishbone while he made her come, spouting filthy endearments at him or at some cuss named Gene. It was tougher to tell when a gal came half in Cherokee.

As he satisfied himself after her and went limp in her love saddle to fight for his second wind, Elvira crooned, ''Oh, thank you, I didn't know how much I needed that. I guess I'd been denying how much I missed my man. I'm sorry I evoked his name while you were being so nice to me, Custis. I didn't mean it as an insult to the here and now of us.''

He kissed her gently and soberly replied, ''I took it as a compliment, ma'am. I know how it feels to grieve for a lost love. On occasion I've been known to indulge a sudden bittersweet memory the same way.''

As he rolled off to sit up and grope on the rug for the smokes in his vest, Elvira archly asked who he'd been pretending she was while he'd tried to split her up the middle with that dangerous concealed weapon he used on unsuspecting women.

Longarm modestly replied, ''Just now you had my undivided attention. If you want the pure truth, by the time I've been with a new friend a week or so, I do catch my mind wandering to other gals I've never had, or old flames that still smolder now and again in the back of my mind. You ladies are right about us horny men. We ought to be whipped with snakes for having such curious natures. But the curious cuss who came up with the wheel or, hell, tasted the first oyster, likely had the same hankering to try somebody new for bedtime.''

He fished out a cheroot, sat up straight to thumbnail a matchhead aflame, and lit the smoke before he added, ''You're ahead of me this afternoon, though. I wasn't thinking about anything but what a swell body you had whilst I was in it just now.''

He swung his bare feet back aboard the bed and cuddled her against him to share the smoke as she confessed, ''I'm glad you're such a plain-spoken man with a roving eye, Custis. I've been craving what we just did since poor Gene, or what was left of him, was laid to rest up the mountain. But even as I lay awake at night, pleasuring myself like a silly schoolgirl, I just dreaded having to croon love words at some man who'd never be my one true love, just because he was fucking me!''

Longarm put the cheroot to her lips as he said, ''I follow your drift. Queen Victoria and the sky pilots want us to combine the two feelings. And when folks manage to combine 'em, the way Her Majesty and her Prince Albert bragged they had, I reckon it's the bee's knees. But they ain't the same feelings. So they don't always go together. A man can love a mother, a daughter, or even a wife to where he'd go down fighting for them like an Arapaho. But that same man may feel like taking on both Thompson brothers over another gal they only want to rut with like a wallowing hog. Since we're being honest to the point of bragging, I may as well confess I still look back in wonder at some high times I've had with downright homely surprises I'd never want my friends to see me on the street with. I suspect a lot of such moments stolen from a mostly short and tedious share of eternity are caused by how hard up we feel and what our original plans for the evening might have been.''

Elvira took a thoughtful drag on the one cheroot and told him it was about time they started making plans, adding it was getting later by the minute.

He stretched luxuriously and said, ''They won't be looking for us before supper time, and we got some more slap and tickle to get out of the way before I take you downstairs to supper. They'll have left me a note at the desk if Doc Maytag wants us to join him this evening to jaw about that shoot-out over at your place. He may hold off until tomorrow if he's planning on an autopsy after closing hours.''

Elvira shuddered and said, ''That's what I mean. We have to make some plans about where we can spend the night more safely, Custis! I know you can protect me here at this hotel during business hours. But what if they come late at night, when there's nobody else around and you could be sound asleep?''

He said, ''I never sleep sound when I'm up against armed owlhoots, and we ain't alone here. We're in a hotel, surrounded by the staff and other guests. Try looking at it from *their* point of view, honey. Would you rather move in on a target on the prod for you if he was hiding in some private home on the outskirts of town, or forted up on the top floor of a transient hotel in the center of town?''

She said, ''I'm not a madwoman sending armed men after you and your friends. I'm a frightened friend and I have friends of my own up in the county seat who'd be willing to shelter me until this all blows over! So why don't I just hide out in Golden until you lawmen catch those wild and crazy-mean outlaws?''

Longarm said, ''Doc Maytag is going to want at least a deposition from both of us about that last shootout. Even if we could get you out of his inquest, there's no coach leaving for Golden this late in the day. The afternoon coach *from* Golden will be arriving most any old time, if it ain't already. But then the crew will lay over here tonight, and drive back in the morning. They were making up the mail bags for that run when I was at the post office earlier.''

She said somebody might be driving north in their own rig, or that she might be able to hire a sulky to drive herself out of town before dark.

He said, ''Honey, you're talking foolish, no offense. If those last members of the gang are still after anybody, the last place you want to be after dark is out on the trail in the dark all alone. You know I can't leave town along with you. You know I got to stay here!''

She tried, "But what if they didn't *know* I was leaving town?"

He snorted and said, "If they ain't watching out for us, you haven't a thing to worry about. If they know where you are, it's still *me* they seem worried about, and by now they should have noticed they'd have been well advised to just leave me alone. They've lost two men in two tries if you count that excitement at your place a try to get me personally."

He took another drag, blew a thoughtful smoke ring, and continued. "If I could figure out why someone in that bunch has such a hard-on for me and me alone, I'd likely have them as good as in the box."

Elvira snuggled closer again as she said, "I don't find that part mysterious, Custis. You have quite a reputation— as a lawman, I mean—and they'd naturally be worried about you catching them."

He shook his head and said, "There has to be more to it than that. The mastermind who planned that post office robbery had to expect a whole slew of lawmen heading this way to catch them. A whole slew did. County deputies swept the surrounding range for sign. Mining company dicks swept empty company property for anyone hiding out after the robbery. Post office inspectors were out here ahead of me. Not a one of those earlier lawmen were attacked by outlaws with Big Fifty buffalo rifles. The outlaws just lay low, the way outlaws are supposed to. Yet they or their possibly female mastermind seems to have gone *loco en la cabeza* at the very notion of this badge toter, and this badge toter alone, riding into Mulligan. And how in blue blazes could they have known I'd be riding into Mulligan before I got here? They were waiting for me along that pony track from Denver. I could have taken the narrow-gauge out of Denver to Golden and come down from the north by coach. How could they have expected me to borrow riding stock from personal pals just outside the Denver city limits? Who could have warned them and why did they *care*?"

She proved she'd been paying attention by saying, "There were four of them with guns we know of, before they were silly enough to mess with you. You met two riding out from Denver. What if the other two were watching the coach road from the north? Don't those numbers add up, and what if they were just worried about *any* federal deputy coming out from the Denver District Court?"

He kissed the part in her dark hair and said, "Your numbers add up if we go with four men and a gal as the original numbers. There could be more or less this long after the robbery. Why *any* of them seem so attached to the scene of their crime is another bone I keep gnawing in vain. But to get back to the second part of your notion, they'd have no more reason to be anxious about a U.S. deputy marshal than a whole bunch of local and postal lawmen. So in all due modesty, it was me in particular they were worried about!"

She kissed his collarbone and murmured, "Small wonder. You've managed to kill half the gang off without knowing who you were after!"

He laughed, said he sure hoped so, and snubbed the smoke to make love to her some more.

It was swell the second time, but Longarm was damned if he didn't start to wondering what it would have been like if he'd taken sassy Cyn Gilliam up on her earlier offer up in Madame Velvet's room. As he braced his weight above the Cherokee breed's tawny torso, admiring the sight of his love-slicked shaft parting the jet black fuzz between her firm thighs, he wondered idly what it might feel like, where it really counted, in the same position with a bigger, softer, paler, and somewhat older but still mighty pretty white gal who, like this one, acted prim and proper in front of men with her clothes on.

Elvira didn't share any of her own lusty daydreams with him as they finished, got cleaned up, dressed, and went downstairs to have an early supper.

Elvira suggested, and Longarm tended to agree, that

townsfolk were less likely to talk if they went out to a restaurant down the street from the hotel at a time when most were on their way home for their own suppers.

The place Elvira chose, being a resident of Mulligan, served plain but wholesome fare at middle-class prices. She said she'd eaten there on happier occasions with her late husband. Then she said she was sorry if that sounded as if she was unhappy about Longarm. She explained she'd meant she hadn't been worried about anyone shooting her through the plate-glass window to her left as she was having supper.

Before Longarm had to come up with a graceful answer, the motherly waitress came over to take their order. She didn't ask what the Widow Tenkiller was doing there with another man. She knew who Longarm was, and allowed they were honored to serve such a famous lawman. So he felt obliged to order their special for the two of them, and they were both glad when that turned out to be roast spring lamb with canned carrots and mashed potatoes, all prepared and served with as much class as you'd find in a Pullman dining car.

Their shoofly pie served with cheddar cheese was good too. They were having their second cup of coffee and talking about that inquest when Undersheriff Babcock illustrated Elvira's concerns about plate glass by spotting them from outside and coming in to join them, taking his hat off to Elvira as he told Longarm, "We found that other pony. The one that cuss you missed rode away on. You'll never guess where it turned up on its own!"

Longarm tried, "The livery stable just up the street?"

The older lawman sighed and said, "Aw, you're no fun and don't be so smug. Every rider knows a livery horse comes home by itself if it knows its oats and the cuss who hired it earlier abandons it to run off on foot. That tethered pony that never got away was from the same livery. So now we have good descriptions if not the true names of all but one of those four who robbed the post office!"

Chapter 16

A busy stable was no place for dainty high-button shoes. So they left Elvira in the care of a junior deputy at Babcock's office while they interviewed the hostlers running the livery service and municipal corral. It was just as well. Babcock turned the air blue with sulfurous curses after he heard a real lawman asking questions he'd never thought to.

Both the tethered pony recovered with a saddle out front of the stationery shop and the abandoned barebacked mount were worn-down cow ponies the local livery had bought cheap to hire out dear. Both were nondescript chestnuts. Both had been hired with bits and bridles they'd been broken to, but without any livery saddles, by one man who answered to the description of the late Pecos Tim Sheehan, one day before Longarm had ridden out from Denver to find at least two of the gang waiting for him out on the range. The one who'd gotten away had obviously done so with the both of them.

Longarm told the older lawman, "They never hired these ponies as getaway mounts at the time of that robbery. The four of them were on foot before and after. With their own private saddles and saddle guns on hand when they somehow learned I was coming and hired two and *only two* ponies to head me off. So there goes the notion they were covering both my likely approaches. They knew I'd be on that pony shortcut out of Denver before I knew so my ownself!"

Babcock cussed some more and said, "I never asked about that because you never told me you hadn't known you were coming. *We* were told you were coming, of course. None of us had been getting anywhere and they said they were sending us a famous tracker. So might you be saying one of my own deputies could be in with them post office robbers?"

Longarm said, "Anything's possible. It's just as likely one of the gang overheard such talk in the Chloride. Your notion about all four of 'em holed up with one hooker makes sense, up to a point. I can't see what could be holding them so tight near the scene of their crimes, *plural*, now that they've tried to kill a government agent on two separate occasions!"

Babcock suggested, "They must know we're expecting them to break cover. They dasn't even send that whore out for food and liquor now that we're watching for her as well, right?"

Longarm grimaced and said, "That's about the size of it. Russian Val and at least one of them who got here first were living more or less respectable up until the time I rode in to upset their apple cart. They sent her to scout my hotel last night. I don't see how they figured I'd figured out she was one of Madame Velvet's whores, but if they hadn't, they'd have never pestered Elvira Tenkiller. Miss Elvira had done sewing for Russian Val. Russian Val knew this. So they sent those two gunslicks to find out what I'd told Miss Elvira, not what she might have told me. They were expecting me to ask Miss Elvira a question about her customer, Russian Val. I sure wish I knew what it was they were so worried about. All Miss Elvira could tell me was that she'd done some sewing for some of Madame Velvet's hookers and that one of them had answered to the handle

125

of Valya Sikorski, better known to the boys at the Chloride as Russian Val. But there must be more for them to worry about than that.''

Babcock frowned thoughtfully and decided, ''They must have thought you, or Miss Elvira, knew more about Russian Val than either of you seem to. All I know is that she was one of Madame Velvet's wilder whores, and I only know that from the talk around town. I can't say I'd know the fallen woman if I saw her on the street.''

Longarm said, ''Miss Elvira describes her as plain to pretty in a short dumpy way. Ash Woodside described her as mousy. According to the late Madame Velvet's diary, she was never there at all. So what we seem to be looking for is a wicked reputation, sort of hanging in midair, like the smile of that Cheshire cat in the tale about Miss Alice.''

Babcock grimaced and declared, ''That makes no sense. Folks come to their doors and windows when a new face appears along Main Street in a town that has no opera house. Russian Val has to look like someone who'd been here a spell before that robbery.''

The older lawman suddenly laughed in a surprisingly boyish manner and said, ''By Allan Pinkerton's beard, I'm starting to get the hang of this eliminating bullshit! But what in blue blazes is it supposed to add up to?''

Longarm shrugged and said, ''Your guess is as good as mine. I have to send a catch-up night letter to my home office as soon as we've settled up with Doc Maytag about that last dead desperado. I'll be wiring the Texas Rangers as well, in case wanted Texas bad men come in sets. Doc may be able to furnish us with more distinguishing marks once he's looked that last body over.''

He stared thoughtfully out the stable door as the late sun flirted from between two higher peaks over yonder as he added, ''Whilst I'm at it, I may as well wire this Russian Orthodox priest I know in Denver. Russian priests are allowed to marry, and this one's wife gives swell parties in the manse of their old onion-domed church out along the

Camp Weld Road. There's a whole bunch of Russian immigrants in the same neck of the woods, so they can walk to church if they've a mind to. My pal, the Russian sky pilot, or his party-giving wife ought to know if Russian Val's a black sheep from their flock.''

Babcock raised a brow. ''A notorious mining-town whore in an onion-domed church?''

Longarm said, ''Fallen women have to fall from someplace, and I just can't come up with another Russian family tree to fall out of. I know it's a long shot. But it'll cost us less than five cents a word if I wire them at night-letter rates and like a fallen woman, a lawman out to backtrack a fallen woman has to start from someplace.''

They thanked the hostlers and went back out in the fresh air, or halfway fresher air, along Main Street. Undersheriff Babcock had been eliminating away on his own. So he was the one who decided, ''The four riders we're certain of arrived by coach with their saddles and other possibles. Had they ridden in on their own ponies, said ponies would have to be somewhere here in Mulligan, and whilst it's possible none of us local lawmen would have spotted four carefully hidden horses, it aint likely, and they'd have had no call to risk hiring those two livery nags of more recent memory, right?''

Longarm said, ''Billy Vail would be proud of you, pard. If the one who got away with his saddle was packing a south-range roper, my Texas Ranger pals ought to be able to tie him in as a known associate of the late Pecos Tim and the cadaver we're still trying to identify. *He'd* left us that one roping saddle with a Mexican throw-rope for sure.''

As they started legging it the short way to Babcock's office in the front of the jailhouse, the undersheriff suddenly brightened and said, ''I just eliminated something! By the time that livery reported their recovered stray and we figured out where the horse we were holding had to belong, we'd naturally gone over that captured saddle in vain. We were cussing about that. We still have the blamed saddle in our own tack room. But the rider you gunned had neither saddlebags nor a bedroll for us to ponder. So don't that mean the four of them eliminated all such sign and stored them away in their local hidey-hole, and ain't that another elimination in its own right?''

Longarm chuckled fondly and said, ''You're learning. Come morning, that coach bound for Golden will be loading mail for its northwards run and they may be too busy to pester. Might be best if I could talk to them this evening, when they won't be as busy, about four strangers with Texas twangs and matching saddles, coming down from the county seat with them just before that post office robbery!''

Old Babcock proved Jefferson County had chosen a local man with care before they'd pinned his gilt badge on. He said, ''Do yourself a favor and question them in the morning. They both have wives up Golden way and gals down this way they don't think we know about. Ain't none of 'em Russian Val or any other whore from Madame Velvet's, before you ask. The jehu stays here in town with an Irish washerwoman only he seems to admire. The shotgun messenger's been screwing a pretty little quadroon who works as a parlor maid for a company bigwig. Don't ask me if her boss has been banging her too. Suffice it to say *she* ain't Russian Val neither, and that coach crew will likely be more willing to jaw with you in the morning sunlight, whilst the depot crew loads up their coach and neither has to explain any female heads on any pillows next to his own, see?''

Longarm soberly replied, ''I stand corrected, and that's another good reason to always let the local lawmen know you're working in their neck of the woods. Do you know what time they commence their north run in the morning?''

The man who lived there said, ''Sure. Eight A.M., the same as always. Seeing it's less than fifteen country miles, with one stage stop midway. So they let everyone sleep late and still get to Golden in time for a noonday dinner. The bigger post office in Golden still has plenty of time to put any outward-bound mail sacks aboard that short-run narrow-gauge to Denver. Take my advice and take your time with that stagecoach crew. It's been a while, and I've noticed that when you press a witness to where he starts to get steamed, he's inclined to just say he don't remember.''

Longarm said he'd noticed the same thing, and agreed it was a long shot that either the driver or his armed guard had been half as interested in paying passengers down below than the strange pussy waiting for them up ahead.

He wondered idly, as he often had before, whether a married-up man looked forward to getting a piece with his lawfully wedded wife after a night in forbidden feathers with a steady mistress. Most any steady routine could get serious. That was another good reason for a man with a badge and a long list of enemies to stay single.

As they approached the jailhouse, with the low sun to the west at their backs and their shadows striding way the hell out ahead of them, Longarm considered how complicated it could get when a man wasn't tired of any of the ladies he was playing with.

It sure beat all how it never seemed to rain but it poured when it came to willing women. He felt certain that had he not known a single gal over here in Mulligan, he'd be facing another night in town alone with his fist and the *Police Gazette* for company. Yet here he was, fixing to hole up for the night with a pretty breed widow who'd just recalled how good it felt, with a Cordelia for sure, and likely a Cyn Gilliam there for the taking a short stroll away, and with old Portia on hand as *another* smoldering ember he could doubtless fan aflame if he could only get her alone without the other's cussing at him. Those French playwrights who made up comical bedroom farces could be writing from personal experience for all he knew. That was likely why he'd never laughed as hard as some at bedroom farces on the wicked stage. He'd had such close calls in real life, and they weren't half as funny when you were the one rolling over the windowsill with your pants down.

As they went inside, they found that deputy assigned to Elvira was reading a dime's worth of *Night Hawk George and His Daring Deeds,* by Colonel Prentice Ingraham, as big a fibber as Ned Buntline. But the gal they'd left in his charge was nowhere to be found.

Once Undersheriff Babcock had run out of dreadful things to call him, the kid calmly replied, "Don't get your bowels in an uproar, Boss. I had no say in the matter. Miss Elvira got to pacing up and down and fuming about night coming on for a spell. Then she made me carry her over to Doc Maytag's drugstore, and when our deputy coroner said he wouldn't be calling her as a witness before, say, noon tomorrow, she like to had a fit. She told Doc she had to get on up to Golden, and asked if she'd be able to get off with a written statement. So seeing she seemed about to piss down a leg, if not both, Doc Maytag said he'd just make up some deposition from the testimony of Longarm here, and she could sign it when she got back from her more important business."

Longarm grimaced and said, "You sure run a tight ship in Jefferson County. But it's no skin off my ass, and I reckon it's no mystery how that last mysterious stranger died."

He smiled thinly as he stared out at the sunset etching the snowfields of the Front Range in gold wire against an orange and purple sky. Then he decided, "Miss Elvira couldn't have told the panel anything I don't know about that shoot-out over on her stairs. I was there and we've . . . talked it over since. But did she say how she meant to make it up the trail to the county seat with night coming on?"

The younger lawman replied, "She said something about catching a ride aboard a notions dray."

He turned to Babcock to add, "You know that dealer who sells ribbons and bows wholesale along Main Street, Boss? Tall drink of water called Dave Goldwater? Him and his halfbreed helper, Cherokee Dick Rogers, were at the drugstore, stocking up on blister salve, when Miss Elvira got to jawing with Dick Rogers in Cherokee. So I can't give you each and every detail. But they gave her time to run over to her place and pack a carpetbag for the trip, and what else can I tell you? Nobody ever told me she was under arrest. They left just a few minutes ago. I reckon you could catch up with them easy enough if it's important. Goldwater's dray is still more than half full of notions he ain't sold yet and even when it's empty, old Dave don't drive like that other gent of the Hebrew persuasion, Ben Hur.''

Babcock told Longarm, "Save you some time if you were to borrow my horse and saddle around to the back.''

Longarm shrugged and replied, "To what end? It's a free country and as our pard here just observed, it ain't as if she just escaped from us. If Doc Maytag ain't in an uproar over her spending the next few days with friends in Golden, why should I pester her to stay?''

Undersheriff Babcock didn't answer. He was getting the hang of this eliminating notion. So he felt no call to mention what a maid from the Drover's Rest had whispered to him about Longarm and Miss Elvira just before he'd found them having supper with their duds back on. It was no skin off Jefferson County's nose if the Widow Tenkiller spent the night with Longarm or not, and it seemed safe to assume Longarm didn't seem too upset about it either. So the poor thing had likely been a dud in bed, and that eliminated one of his own dirty daydreams while they were at it. It sure beat all how scientific methods could save a lawman's brain power for more serious woolgathering.

Chapter 17

Longarm dropped by the Drover's Rest in the unlikely event Elvira had left a message there for him. She hadn't. But the desk clerk gave him a scented envelope from the Gilliam sisters. It invited him to an open house buffet at eight, and said they'd invited some other important gents he might like to know.

He'd been planning on holing up for the night at the Drover's Rest with or without Elvira Tenkiller. Spending the night with the heirs of Madame Velvet and their lawyer promised to be risky for them and sticky for him, whether those outlaws made another try for him or not. There was no graceful way to spend the night under the same roof with a lawyer you'd slept with, a client you'd slept with, and another client who wanted to sleep with you. But he wanted to return that blank volume, and he had some other questions about it. So he took the time to have a hot bath and a shave, change his shirt as well as his socks, and drop by the Western Union to send a whole raft of longer than usual wires at night-letter rates.

He was still a tad early when he finally anbled on over to Madame Velvet's with that one leather-bound volume under his arm. Old Gus, pretending to be a butler, let him in and showed him to the parlor, which had recenty been a whorehouse taproom. The older man's wife was presiding over the buffet lined up along the top of the bar. That was what you called a saloon's free lunch when you served the boiled eggs, cold cuts, and such at home, a buffet.

The ladies hadn't come down yet, there were only three gents at hand thus far, and you weren't supposed to dig in to a buffet ahead of the pack. So Longarm was glad he'd had that early supper when he saw they expected him and those other three early arrivals to nurse tall glasses of rum punch with just enough gin to remind a man he could use a drink.

Longarm knew Ash Woodside from the post office, of course. So Ash introduced him to the other two. Once he had, Longarm saw what they were doing there early.

A potbellied old fart with an iron-gray beard and a brocaded vest worth twice what Longarm paid for his suits was one of the partners who owned and operated that shortline stagecoach based in Golden. As they shook, Longarm refrained from telling him he'd heard the stage line wanted to buy the whorehouse for a hotel, or what he'd heard about their jehu and shotgun messenger in Mulligan between runs. The vested interest's name was Dennis Phalen, and he made no bones about having known Madame Velvet of old, although over Georgetown way when both of them had been younger and less respectable. He said he'd been pained to hear such a grand blow job had died, but business was business and this was a swell location for a resort hotel. That was what you called such a place in the mountains close to Denver once the only mine for miles around bottomed out, a resort hotel.

The other punch drinker was introduced as one Merlin Oberon from back East, if not from under a mushroom. He was a consumptive dapper spectacle in lavender-gray broadcloth who shook hands like a dead woman, and Longarm had seldom met grown men who used henna rinse on their hair. Oberon said he was a literary agent. That was likely the reason for the swishy fake name. It turned out both of them had come in that afternoon on the same stage-coach and been invited to stay the night by the Gilliam sisters, seeing they'd both come on business with the sisters.

It was the gruffer Dennis Phalen who noted the leather-bound book with DIARY stamped in copper on its fake alligator cover and asked if that was by any chance the famous diary of Madame Velvet that they'd said so much about.

Longarm handed it over, saying, "Just one volume. Blank. I brought it back after showing it to somebody else today. They were talking about it up around the county seat?"

Phelan shook his head and said he'd only learned of its existence on the way down from Golden with his newfound friend Oberon.

The literary agent explained, "I came out west from Chicago to see for myself. Now that I have, I fear I came on a fool's errand. Portia Parkhurst, their attorney, left me alone with some volumes this very afternoon when we first got here, and I must say this Madame Velvet led a rather astounding life!"

"She sucked cock like a weaning calf," said Phalen with a sigh. He added, "I don't care if there's anything in there about me when me and the world was young and a good-looking white woman was worth ever' damn dime she demanded. I'm sort of proud that I could come three or four times a night in those days, and since I never married, it's no skin off my nose if Madame Velvet said she blew my French horn on more than one occasion!"

Merlin Oberon repressed a shudder and said, "Speak for yourself. A lot of lusty young pioneers did go on to wed girls from back East and raise a second generation they could afford to send to college. I told Miss Portia right off that no publisher I can think of would buy memoirs such as those to be sold as true stories over the counter!"

Longarm nodded and said, "Great minds seem to run

along the same channels. I told her much the same, riding as I do out of the Denver District Court. Less modest men than Mister Phelan here would do most anything to see their wilder days in early Colorado remained a faded memory of the past.''

Ash Woodside, the postmaster of a still fairly rugged mining town, was the one who asked, ''Why not publish the dirty diary as fiction, to be sold in secret, with the real names changed to protect the guilty?''

The literary agent pursed his prissy lips. ''What might ten percent of small change amount to? The only people who make money from pornography are the dealers in such smut. Writers of any talent who pen such classics as the *Confessions of a French Maid* do so as a labor of lust or in the mistaken belief one can attain fame and fortune as that great author Anonymous. People willing to pay real money to read smut want real smut about real people. Or smut made up about real people. That recent exposé of the late Brigham Young, by an imaginative young thing claiming to be a runaway Mormon bride, can only be sold openly because she was careful not to say anything really *dirty* about the dirty old man she was forced to share with all those other Mormon wives.''

He struck a pose as he added knowingly, ''You can beat about the bush, naming names, without any slurping noises or exact details of their depravities, or you can sell really interesting perversions on the part of people so depraved the reader doesn't care to know who they really were, see?''

Longarm said, ''I reckon. You're talking about books like *Justine* by de Sade, where a made-up degenerate gal named Justine likes to kill her fool self trying to come up with dirtier deeds than anyone has ever done before, right?''

Oberon minced, ''Exactly. De Sade had a lot more imagination than our poor Madame Velvet. Or perhaps the poor old bawd was recording the simple truth. Whether she and her girls served those suddenly flush young pioneers as she boasts, or whether she made some of the wilder details up, her diary is simply too dirty to publish as the truth, and not *different* enough to publish as pornography.''

Dennis Phelan chuckled lewdly and observed, ''Many an old pal might be relieved to hear that, Mr. Oberon. Albeit I ain't ashamed if you got to a night where I got sucked off by Buck-Toothed Alice after I'd been prospecting all week over by Silver Plume.''

The motherly old woman presiding over her cooling buffet suddenly turned to leave the room, red-faced and walking as fast as if she had to take a sudden shit.

Longarm said, ''I remember when Georgetown was booming. That was where they had that famous saloon sign, wasn't it?''

Phelan just laughed, sort of smug.

Oberon said, ''I don't think I read that far back, once I'd seen how a certain state senator of today admired spicy Mexican dishes. I mean, I suppose some men find dusky *señoritas* a novelty, and I suppose you'd call eating any pussy a common courtesy. But a bowl of Mexican *shit*, served with chili peppers and tortillas, with her under the table to suck you off as you enjoy such a meal? I mean . . . really!''

Phelan laughed easily and suggested, ''Don't say you don't like something before you've tried it. But to tell the pure truth, I never knew Miss Chihuahua Rose served bowls of her exotic shit to the customers.''

Longarm's eyes met those of the disgusted-looking postmaster. Longarm said, ''They never sent me all this way to look into the favorite foods of future senators that far back in the mists of time. They're really worried about more recent events. I suspect I know who that mousy gal was. But I didn't find any mention of that Russian Val who seems to have had a hand in that robbery you suffered. Still trying to figure out what she could have done here that was too filthy for Madame Velvet to record. Seems an old

136

whore who'd confess to serving literal filth to customers would have put down anything Russian Val could have done to get fired."

Ash suggested, "What about a serious felony? A crime that could have put Madame Velvet out of business before she could die? If that mousy little thing who fingered us for that robbery was Russian Val, it's an established fact she's capable of armed robbery and an associate of known killers."

Old Phelan nodded and volunteered, "Madame Velvet was ever straight with the boys, and ran a decent whorehouse where nobody was likely to get robbed or assaulted on the premises. So say this Russian Val put her hand on someone's money or a knife in someone's back, wouldn't a whore *that* dirty be drummed out of the corps and scratched off all the duty rosters?"

Before Longarm could answer, the Gilliam sisters came down the grand staircase, followed by Portia Parkhurst, the three of them visions in spring evening wear of crisp pastel organdy. Pale blue in the case of Portia, and matched blushing-rose in the case of the Gilliam gals.

So after they'd all had their wrists kissed, it was all right to dig into the buffet, and that old lady even came back out to serve them from behind the counter. Longarm wound up in a corner with Portia and the Swedish meatballs she'd vouched for while other guests arrived. All male, as Portia observed with a sniff about small-town mores and stuck-up mining-camp wives.

Longarm tried to soothe her. "They're as likely scared as stuck up, Miss Portia. We *are* standing in the parlor of a house of ill repute, and the ladies of Mulligan likely sent their menfolk on ahead to get the lay of the land before they respond personally to any invites from the Gilliam gals. I can introduce you to them two gents who just came in, if you like. The shorter one's Undersheriff Babcock and the somewhat older and taller cuss would be Doc Maytag, the deputy coroner who runs the drugstore down on Main Street.''

The lady lawyer said to eat his meatballs, and asked if he planned on staying the night up in Madame Velvet's room again.

He shook his head and said, ''Drover's Rest. Room 2-E, if you'd care to join me later. You heard about me shooting it out with that same bunch again earlier today, of course?''

She said, ''Of course. But why should that make me want to join you at your hotel later tonight? A girl's reputation could really suffer keeping company with such a ruffian, Custis Long!''

He smiled sheepishly and replied, ''I warned you I was no good the first night we . . . kept company. My reasons for forting up at the hotel have nothing to do with my more romantic side. The Drover's Rest is just a better fort. One stairway up from a usually fairly crowded lobby, with my room at one end of the straight field of fire down the long corridor. But then best of all, they know which room I'm booked into. They sent one of their gals to ask whilst I was out.''

Portia frowned and asked, ''That's supposed to be best of all?''

He nodded and said, ''I don't have to worry about nobody but them and me. Like I keep telling my boss when he tries to saddle me with another deputy to back my play, I feel more free to play when I ain't concerned with aiming the wrong way in a confusing situation. Poor old James Butler Hickok never lived down the night he shot his pal, Mike Williams, in the process of gutshooting Phil Coe in Abilene. Hickok was under the impression it was a private fight betwixt him and Coe. Had Mike Williams stayed out of it, he'd have surely lived through it. I don't want them outlaws coming after me in a house full of innocent young ladies, not knowing which door I might be behind.''

Portia sniffed and said, ''I'll be the judge of how innocent anyone is around here. Which one of the Gilliam sisters were you reading that bedtime story to when I came up to tuck you in last night?''

Longarm laughed and said, ''Never mind, and you just illustrated my reasons for staying at the hotel. It's too easy to sneak around this big old empty pile.''

''Are you denying you were up to your old tricks with one or more of my clients last night?'' she insisted.

He said, ''I was reading the dirty diary of their dirty old aunt. I fear some of her bad habits must run in the family. But I never went looking for any slap and tickle with anybody, no offense. So about my hired love nest at the Drover's Rest later on . . .''

She laughed despite herself, told him he was awful, and left him there to go jaw with that literary agent.

Longarm wasn't jealous. It was hard to imagine Merlin Oberon doing anything wicked to a woman. Longarm suspected he was what those alientists who studied such matters called a catamite, or a girly-boy who didn't do anything to anyone, but just *took* it. So it was hard for anybody but a born bully to feel anything but gentle contempt for the arty cuss.

Longarm ambled over to the bar to try some chopped goose liver on bitty squares of toast, along with deviled eggs dyed in beet juice and given clove stems to look like plums, even though they were nice spicy eggs. He was joined by Ash Woodside and the undersheriff, who wanted him to settle an argument.

Old Babcock thought those outlaws had stayed on in Mulligan after robbing the post office around Mayday because they meant to do the same around the first of June, when the post office safe would be primed to cash money orders coming in and amassing more as lots of local folks bought money orders to send back East.

The white-haired but husky postmaster said that seemed ridiculous, explaining, ''They caught us by surprise last time. Next time we'll have some extra hands with guns

139

staying on a spell after they deliver the extra funds.''

He patted a bulge under his frock coat of dark broadcloth and added, ''On top of that, the post office has issued me and young Fred Waller, my assistant, the same Colt .38 Lightnings, with sawed-off barrels, packed by plainclothes hands for Railway Express. So just you wait and see what happens if those sons of bitches try to rob us a *second* time!''

Longarm washed down some right nice deviled eggs with insipid rum punch and decided, ''I can't afford to wait and see what may or may not happen at the end of the month. My boss is going to give me holy Ned if I don't wrap this case up a lot sooner than that!''

Undersheriff Babcock said, ''I don't see how. Unless they're dumb enough to come at you some more. What if they just lay low, wherever they've been hiding?''

Longarm shrugged and said, ''I reckon in that case I'll just have to figure out where they've been hiding, won't I?''

Chapter 18

By nine or so the parlor had crowded some, with leading merchants and the top management of the mine up the slope. So Longarm slipped out and up the stairs to Madame Velvet's chambers with that one blank volume. He put it back where it belonged, and lit the lamp on the old whore's writing desk. He had the first of the nineteen volumes and the last one she'd never finished open, side by side, when old Merlin Oberon wafted in, smelling of violet toilet water and pomade.

The literary agent minced, "So there you are. I've been dying to get you alone, ah, Custis."

Longarm quietly replied, "How come? It's only fair to warn you I'm queer for women. I've been trying to fight it all my life, but I just can't help myself."

The limp-wristed dude laughed easily and said, "Don't be silly. Do the flowers chase the bees? I wanted to ask you about that joke you shared with Dennis Phalen downstairs. Something about an unusual saloon sign in some mining town?"

Longarm smiled uncertainly but answered without hesitation. "Over in Georgetown near Idaho Springs. Sign above the saloon door bragged that they sold the worst whiskey, wine, and cigars west of the wide Missouri."

Oberon scowled, not a pretty sight, and said he didn't get it.

Longarm explained, "Sign painter's revenge. The tightwad who owned the saloon argued about the price, in the middle of a silver boom, when he could neither read nor write. So the sign painter advertised him as a dealer in the worst whiskey, wine, and so forth for the price they'd agreed on. The joke backfired. By the time the illiterate saloon keeper found out what the sign really said, he'd done so much business with it reading the way it did that he decided to just leave it be. Don't matter *how* bad your whiskey and wine may be during a boom when many an old boy in from the diggings still *wants* some."

Oberon's scowl got really ugly as he pouted, "Very amusing, I am sure. So why did Dennis Phalen just tell me that sign read that they served the warmest beers and queers in Colorado?"

Longarm shrugged and said, "Maybe he couldn't read himself. Many a man came West after the war with a poor education. I know this for a fact, albeit I was able to read that saloon sign the first time I laughed at it, six or eight years ago."

Oberon cocked a brow—that wasn't pretty either—and minced, "I'm supposed to buy an illiterate owning and operating his own stage line? You seem to be a decent live-and-let-live sort, Deputy Long, so let me tell you something you might not know about the sort who tease and bully my sort. You've heard that it takes a thief to catch a thief? Well—"

Longarm cut him off. "I ain't that illiterate, Mr. Oberon. I've read articles by this alienist from Vienna Town about some gents acting most disgusted about notions they're secretly tempted by. And Phelan did confess right out that he used to know Madame Velvet as one of her customers during the Georgetown rush. At silver strike prices, one has to be feeling sort of desperate before he heads for any whorehouse, and hard-up gents up in the hills with no pocket jingle get to sort of strumming their own banjos and, if the truth be known, experimenting with the sins of Sodom with other broke and lonesome boys.''

Longarm ran a finger down across the spidery handwriting in the two volumes, from one to the other, as he added, ''Some men can pluck life's forbidden fruits or leave 'em be. Others feel the need to beat up anyone who's led them down the primrose path, or *tempted* them to *follow* it. But you surely know by now that the rider in the bunch a gent like you has to worry about is the youngest cowboy with the most girlish face.''

It had been a statement rather than a question. So the catamite soberly replied, ''Gee, I wish you weren't so set in your own ways. So in what volume might Madame Velvet have recorded the sickening sex life of our ever-so-masculine stage-line operator?''

Longarm thought and decided, ''Volume six to nine ought to cover her days in Georgetown during the rush of the late '60's. The years '67 and '68 were the peak of the boom when a prospector working solo could still get rich. By '69 they'd brought in power drills and the mines were being run as business ventures, like the one in this town. I ain't got time to go through all these volumes entry by entry, but if you want the bother, I suspect you'll find a younger Dennis Phalen making a lucky strike and selling out to one of the big mining moguls. He'd be running a mining company instead of a stage line if he'd stayed in that business. He'd have never had the money to start up or buy out a stage line if he'd never had any luck at all as a mining man. We call what I'm doing eliminating. I ain't worried about Dennis Phalen's past or present. They sent me out this way to catch a gang of *robbers*. I can't *like* anybody sporting a vest like that either, but he ain't on my list of logical suspects, and nothing he might have done with his dick during a silver strike in another neck of the woods sounds like a federal offense to this child.''

Oberon said, ''Speak for yourself. I told you some of the

entries I've read so far are dynamite! What are you looking for if you don't care about anyone's past sex lives?''

Longarm closed both volumes and rose to place them back where they belonged as he said, ''Making sure they were made by the same bookbinder and comparing the handwriting, early and late. I *am* interested in a suspect who's reputed to have worked downstairs as one of Madame Velvet's whores. They called her Russian Val, and said she liked it up her ass by the way.''

Oberon sniffed and complained, ''Why do you he-men always assume you know so much about the personal habits of people you refuse to go to bed with? Didn't you just say the love that dare not speak its name was not a federal offense?''

Longarm turned from putting the volumes back with the others over the writing table and replied, ''She ain't wanted in connection with her ports of entry. I want to question her about a post office robbery as *does* come under our jurisdiction.''

Leaving the limp-wristed literary agent alone with the diary of Madame Velvet, Longarm made his way downstairs, or tried to. Alone on an upper landing, he was waylayed by Cyn Gilliam, the older of the two sort of sporty spinsters, who dragged him off the stairs by one sleeve as she whispered, ''Custis, we have to talk!''

They paid him to poke his nose into private matters, so he allowed he was all ears as they wound up in what had to have been one of the upstairs cribs when the place had been a going concern. There was just room to turn around in, with a sort of institutional bedstead, framed with steel tubing painted pink, taking up most of the space under a hanging lamp someone had surely lit since Madame Velvet had been out of business. The sheet, singular, and two pillows on the bed were a more shocking shade of pink sateen. Cyn Gilliam closed the door after them and threw the bolt, saying, ''It's about my little sister. I have reason to believe she's no longer a virgin.''

144

Longarm chose his words with care, knowing women bragged more about their romantic conquests than men. When a man got laid he bragged as if he'd won a turkey shoot. When a woman got laid she *confessed,* to everyone who'd listen, that she'd been swept off her innocent feet by a handsome cuss who just couldn't resist her charms. So if Cordelia hadn't told her big sister they'd spent a night together up in Madame Velvet's feather bed, Cordelia was a freak of nature as well as a sex maniac.

Hoping this was true, Longarm cautiously replied, "That well may be, Miss Cyn, but I fail to see what you expect me to *do* about it. As a mere mortal man, I only know how to help a young lady get *rid* of her virginity. I've no idea how you'd go about putting it *back,* and if you mean to imply I had anything to do with your kid sister's loss of innocence, I stand willing to swear I was not the dastardly knave who first cut that cake!"

This was the simple truth as soon as you studied on it. Cordelia had made the first moves upstairs, and he was getting another hard-on just thinking back to how she'd moved her experienced little tailbone.

Cyn sighed and said, "I suspect I'm partly to blame for letting her in on our family secrets. My notorious name-sake, Aunt Cynthia, or Madame Velvet, used to behave like a grand lady when she came home to Wichita now and again for family weddings, funerals, and such. So only our dear old dad, her younger brother, knew where the money she sent home now and again really came from. But alas, Dad told me just before he died a few summers back, and I like a fool confided in Cordelia, lest something happen to me and I take the secret to my grave. Aunt Cynthia was still alive, you see, and I was afraid she'd sweep in out of the golden West and shock a child unprepared for some of the things she could say, late in the evening after a few nips of tonic."

Longarm said, "Lots of families have such awkward se-crets, and they lead to awkward feelings no matter how they

145

may be dealt with. Why are you taking my gun belt off, Miss Cyn?''

She said, ''I lost my virginity to a preacher man in Wichita I'll ever be grateful to. But I never knew, till I read that scandalous diary upstairs, how wild and wicked the forbidden pleasures of the flesh could be! I confess I'd tried most all the suggestions in the Song of Solomon with one preacher man or another over the years. But when I think of the years I've wasted at just plain fornication, with my chemise or nightgown on, in the damned *dark*! I want to do it as if I was one of the whores who used to work here and you were a mining man who hadn't seen a woman for months! I want you to strip me down naked as a jay and rut with me like a hog! I hope you didn't take a bath before you came here this evening. You smell suspiciously of bay rum!''

Longarm laughed and said he was sorry he didn't smell bad or need a shave. And by this time she'd shucked that rose organdy dress with an ease a real whore might have envied, and as she threw her stark naked form across the shocking pink sateen, moaning for him to hurry, Longarm could only reflect on how they expected him to investigate anything suspicious in the vicinity of that post office. They were less than a quarter mile from said post office, and she was certainly acting a mire unusual for a gal who'd claimed to be a Kansas shopkeeper. So he hung up some of his stuff, let anything he couldn't find a hook for look after itself, and mounted her stark naked to decide that, all in all, there was little to choose between the Gilliam sisters. The two of them were blessed with passionate twats, and neither needed any lessons in the art of gyrating her hips.

But thanks to the lamplight shining down on her writhing nude body, Longarm could see the older sister was commencing to get a mite thicker around the waist, although with bigger tits almost as firm as those of her sassy kid sister. And if Cordelia was just a tad prettier, Cyn had a somewhat tighter grip on the situation down yonder. So a good time was had by all, and trying to decide which of them was the best lay made for an even better time as he toyed with the notion of three-in-a-tub while he gave his all to good old Cyn.

He *thought* that was all she wanted, until he'd rolled off spent to suggest a breather, only to discover she was just getting started. She allowed her late aunt's dirty diary had opened her mind to new horizons. He had to laugh as he asked whether that was her *mind* she was trying to take his semi-erection in to the roots. He was sure it was aimed more down her throat than up into her brain as she commenced to bob her head up and down without answering.

Then she wanted him to Greek her, but he convinced her that dog-style, while watching their reflections in the window glass near the bed, was just as sassy a position and not as dangerous to her innards. She agreed, once he got really going that way, that she was just as glad it wasn't that far up her actual ass.

When she finally had mercy on him and he was able to consult his pocket watch, he was surprised, as ever, by how much a couple could accomplish in less than a full hour if they really put their genitals to it. So the party was still going on in the parlor when Longarm was able to slip out the back door and sneak through the moonlit garden and around to Mine Road. It was a balmy evening for that time of the year in the Front Range. But he sniffed in vain for the odors of licorice or anise. That was the trouble with reading sign. You always came across sign that might or might not mean anything, as if a bird dog sniffing for pheasant caught the scent of a rabbit. Neither had to be a false scent. But like a good bird dog, you were supposed to neither miss any sign nor follow sign that didn't lead anywhere.

Striding down the dark Mine Road to a Main Street not much lighter at this hour, Longarm told himself to stop thinking about anything but the one thing he'd managed to decide on, back where he'd just been. He was sure all nineteen volumes of the diary of Madame Velvet had been made by the same bookbinder, if not marketed by the same mail-order house, and kept from volume one to the unfinished volume nineteen in the same spidery hand. So why in thunder didn't Russian Val's name show up a single time if Madame Velvet had kept records on such customers as old Dennis Phalen?

And how come Dennis Phalen hadn't chosen to tell Oberon, or been unable to tell Oberon, about that famous saloon sign in Georgetown if he'd really known Georgetown during its wild and woolly silver boom of the late '60's? And why was Longarm reading that fool sign to *himself* in the dark, as if it was hanging across Mine Road like a street banner, for Pete's sake?

The fool sign had never made that much of an impression on him the first time he'd noticed it one afternoon in Georgetown, before he'd learned how tough it was to make money up in the hardrock mines and taken Billy Vail up on a chance to ride for Uncle Sam. That had all been years ago, and the only point to the weak joke was that a man who couldn't read had no idea what was hanging above his door in plain sight.

So what if Dennis Phalen himself hadn't been able to remember the point of the joke because he, like that saloon owner, hadn't been able to *read* the fool sign?

"I can ask him," Longarm decided, breaking step but not turning back as he considered whether turning around and walking all the way back was worth it.

He'd decided it could wait until the next time they met up. But a man breaking step in the moonlight makes a tricky target, and so when that Sharps .50-170 roared in the night like a bolt of dry lightning, its snarling seven-hundred-grain slug missed Longarm's right ear by a whisker as it passed through the shade of his moonlit hat brim.

Chapter 19

As the loud rifle shot echoed away, windows opened and dogs barked while Longarm hunkered for a million years behind the picket fence he'd vaulted. When nothing else happened, he worked his way through backyards to Main Street, and entered his hotel through a side door.

When he asked at the desk, that mysterious mousy gal hadn't been by to ask where he was this time. The sons of bitches had doubtless heard about that buffet most of the bigwigs in town had been invited to in writing.

Longarm knew both the Choride Saloon and Western Union would still be open. He headed for the Western Union to steady his nerves before he turned in for the night. A man who steadied his nerves in a lamplit saloon when he knew someone was gunning for him was a man who wasn't experienced in such matters.

Longarm kept an eye on the door, and stayed out of line with the front windows as he stood at the Western Union counter, composing night letters they said they'd deliver early the next business day.

So that was where Undersheriff Babcock caught up with him, saying, ''Figured you might be here when you weren't at the Drover's Rest or the Chloride. Was that you they fired that cannon at a few minutes ago and if so, who are you wiring about it?''

Longarm handed the last of his night letters over to the telegraph clerk behind the counter and told Babcock, ''I mentioned that latest try in my catch-up report to my home office. But I'm more interested in some other queries I just got off, including informal requests for information from Emma Gould and Ruth Jacobs over Denver way.''

Babcock proved he was a Colorado rider by raising a brow to demand, ''You figure the two most notorious whores of Denver can tell us who just pegged a shot at you on the streets of Mulligan?''

Longarm shook his head and explained, ''I'll be mighty surprised if that same .50-170 ain't still in the possession of a whore-lover hiding out and mayhaps taking orders or serious suggestions from that mysterious Russian Val. So I've asked some important dealers in pussy out our way what they can tell me about Russian Val, Chop Suey Sally, and, oh, yeah, Creole Annie, a lady of color who specializes in what they call *sesenta y nueve* or *al reverso* along the border, where Latin notions are offered more often.''

Babcock whistled and said, ''Madame Velvet expected gents to go sixty-nine with a colored whore? I didn't even know she had any gals like so whoring for her! If I had, I'd have had to have put a stop to it. You know that even fucking a gal of an inferior race is against state law, and you ain't supposed to commit crimes against nature with *white* gals!''

Longarm quietly replied, ''So I've heard. They usually say colored gals working in Colorado whorehouses are just house servants, and I've read the Leadville city ordinance regarding Chinese. Whether that may be constitutional or not ain't the question before the house here in Mulligan. My only interest in the late Madame Velvet lies in her odd written records of the recent past. I haven't been able to find anyone who recalls Chinese or colored gals working there when the diary-keeping Madame Velvet died. Yet she records their mighty sassy antics with more than one local bigwig and a state senator I've seen under that capitol dome in Denver.''

Babcock suggested, ''Mayhaps they don't want it known they got down and dirty with this Chop Suey Sally and Creole Annie. I know *I* sure wouldn't.''

Longarm said, ''I hadn't finished. There ain't a single entry about a Russian Val who takes it up the ass. Yet more than one gent I've met here in Mulligan *recalls* such a gal. Taking it up the ass for a slightly higher fee at Madame Velvet's. Does that make sense to you?''

The older lawman shook his head and said, ''Nope. But try her another way. What if Chop Suey Sally and Creole Annie were *code words* for her specialists in crimes against nature? Madame Velvet had been in the fucking business for going on twenty years. So she'd have known as well as you and me that *written proof* could get corn-holing and cock-sucking gals put away for at least a year at hard.''

Longarm said, ''That's why I wired some experts on the subject. To eliminate Chop Suey Sally and Creole Annie as real whores. If Madame Velvet changed names now and again to protect her gals, she sure didn't give a shit about her *customers.* Looking for some reference to Russian Val, I caught some of your most respected married men in Mulligan going down on Chop Suey Sally. According to Madame Velvet, she'd only let a man get really wild with her if he was willing to loosen her up with his tongue. She said it proved he really liked her.''

The older lawman laughed wickedly and said, ''I've heard tell that after a man's et Chinee pussy he wants some *more* in a little while. I'll ask around town and see if I can find someone who'll admit any memories of any Chinese or colored gals working yonder. You'd expect some old boy to at least recall them from the taproom downstairs, if they don't want to admit being *upstairs* with either!''

They shook on that and parted friendly. Longarm slipped back to his hired room at the Drover's Rest, found the match stem he'd wedged in a bottom door hinge still in place, and removed the mattress from the bedstead to turn in forted up in a corner behind a chest of drawers he'd shifted. That wasn't the first night he'd spent in a hotel with unknown enemies somewhere around town.

The next morning he put everything back the way he'd found it and enjoyed an early breakfast, fried eggs over chili con carne, before he moseyed over to the stage depot to see that, sure enough, young Fred Waller from the post office was loading mailbags in the northbound's boot with the help of a depot hand. The coach stood unhitched in a side alley. The front entrance of the depot faced Main Street. The six-mule team, slated to haul the coach north, had been harnessed but left around the back until they were ready to leave because mules hitched up to pull anything got proddy just standing there and not pulling. To Longarm's experienced eye, they'd already been harnessed longer than an army wagon master would have allowed for.

Longarm saw neither the jehu nor his shotgun messenger anywhere out of doors that morning. So he moseyed inside to see if that might be where they were.

They weren't. A middle-aged woman dressed sort of country sat at one end of the waiting room bench with her carpetbag and a gunnysack full of something lumpy. Merlin Oberon, the literary agent, perched at the far end with a travel duster over his gorgeous duds and a pigskin overnight case near his high-button shoes.

He held out a limp hand as Longarm came over to ask how things had gone with that book deal over on Mine Road.

Oberon made a wry face and said, "Too rich for my blood as a true confession. Not imaginative enough as pornography. As I told the sisters, I fail to see why their aunt bothered writing page after page of what was, after all, the same old grind, night after night and year after year. You he-men who consider such establishments the depths of depravity have no imagination at all. I could take you to private clubs in Frisco or Saint Lou that would really set you free. But alas, I suppose that's too much to hope for!''

Longarm smiled thinly and said, ''Blame it on my upbringing. Is old Dennis Phalen staying on here in Mulligan?''

Oberon shook his head and replied, ''That's why they're taking their own sweet time outside. After a good night's sleep and an interminable breakfast, he asked me, of all people, to tell them the coach wouldn't be leaving before nine.''

The older woman jumped to her feet, exclaiming, ''Aroo! I can't wait until any damned nine! Sure I have to be in Golden before noon!''

Oberon said, ''Don't blame me, my dear woman. I agree the owner of this line is a self-indulgent pig.''

She went storming outside with her heavy load to fuss at the crew.

Oberon sniffed and said, ''I wonder what she had in that gunnysack. It looked like cabbages. Did you catch the paddy brogue?''

Longarm said, ''I can see why she's upset. What do you reckon old Phelan is up to back at the whorehouse?''

Oberon shrugged and said, ''Dickering. He's not the only one who's offered to buy the property. The owners of your hotel, the Drover's Rest, and the mining company here in Mulligan have tendered their own offers, according to Miss Parkhurst. Have you ever *had* any of that, by the way? She speaks of you rather wistfully, as if you were an old flame or somebody she was planning to invite to a wedding.''

Longarm said, ''Never mind how their lawyer might or might not like me. Tell me more about old Phelan's plans for their property.''

Oberon said, ''In a nutshell, he's a cheap bastard as well as a self-indulgent pig. Last night, at that gathering, he topped the offers made by the owners of the one hotel and a mining company magnate whose wife has always wanted a place that big. But then at breakfast he told the Gilliam girls and their pretty lawyer that he wanted time to think about an offer he may have made after a couple of sips too many. That was when I left. This whole piggy business is just too distressing. First they want me to get them big money for the scrawled confessions of a dreary old slut, and now they're arguing the worth of a shut-down whorehouse in a fading mining town. I just can't wait to get back to civilization!''

Longarm moved over to a side window overlooking the alley, where that coach now stood untended and forlorn, loaded up for the run but waiting on its big froggy to show up in his fancy vest.

Longarm decided, ''The crew would have been here long ago on a less undecided morning. I'll bet the jehu and his shotgun messenger are up at Madame Velvet's, waiting on their lord and master.''

The literary agent said, ''No bet. He's probably expecting them to carry him over here piggyback. It must be over a furlong, and it took me *minutes* to get here with my baggage.''

Longarm chuckled and said, ''Rank has its privileges. So I reckon that accounts for the ways some struggle to get ahead in this world.''

Oberon proved he followed Longarm's drift by wistfully volunteering, ''If only such struggles didn't change us so. I looked our Dennis up in those volumes you suggested, back in the boom of '68 when he, Madame Velvet, and the world were younger. I was hoping he'd been interested in certain vices, but alas, he just dropped by now and then to have a few drinks and get laid. Madame Velvet wrote fondly of him in the very few passages devoted to such a dull thud. As one might expect, Madame Velvet and her girls were amused by his delusions of glory about his virile member and more impressed by his prowess as a prospector. You would never know it to look at him today, but barely a handful of years back his beard was black, his belly was flatter, and he was still willing to part with a buck.''

Longarm brightened as he caught a flash of that brocaded vest down Main Street, headed his way under an iron-gray beard, between two men dressed more in keeping with an honest day's work.

Behind him, the dude who'd been reading up on the coaching tycoon droned on. "Madame Velvet's last entry about him was just a tad bitter and illustrates what we were talking about. Seems he hadn't been by for a while, and she'd learned he'd stuck a rich silver vein up in the hills. Sold out to some syndicate moving in with air drills and other serious equipment, and left the Georgetown fields without ever coming by for a last fling. She wrote, and I fear I agree, he could probably afford to rut with opera singers, ballet dancers, and such once he'd struck it rich."

Longarm headed for the door, saying, "That's his business. I want to ask his coach crew if they recall four passengers packing saddles and dressed for Texas riding, coming down from Golden with no ponies of their own. No offense, but that was who they sent me over here to look for."

Longarm stepped outside, and started slowly drifting along the boardwalk to meet old Dennis Phelan and his younger employees. The owner of the coach line recognized Longarm at a distance and waved. So Longarm waved back.

As he did so a voice to his rear yelled, "Longarm! Duck!" as all hell busted loose!

Longarm had no handy place to duck, so he crashed sideways through the glass window near the corner of the stage depot as hot lead hummed like a bee through the space his shoulder blades had just been in. As he landed on one shoulder amid a shower of busted glass inside and rolled, Longarm heard a fusillade of lighter-caliber shots out front. So he had his own .44-40 out as he rolled back up to his considerable height and yelled, "Stay put, Mr. Oberon!"

"Who's moving? Who's moving?" screamed the literary agent in a girlish voice as Longarm tore out the door a second time, facing the other way with his six-gun in hand.

He saw young Fred Waller from the post office down at the far end of the stage depot, a smoking Colt Lightning in hand. Between the two of them, facedown across a roping saddle under a thinning haze of gun smoke, sprawled the limp remains Longarm recognized as those of that one who'd gotten away the day before after falling down Elvira Tenkiller's stairs. He was wearing the same worn trail duds. His high-crowned Texas hat lay upside down on the plank walk near his still-smoking Schofield .45.

Fred Waller called anxiously, "Don't shoot! I'm on your side!"

Longarm called back, "I noticed. I didn't think he shot *himself* in the back just now!"

The postal clerk protested, "I had to shoot him in the back! He was turned your way, aiming at *your* back!"

Longarm said, "I said I'd noticed, and I'm much obliged, Fred. You have my word that should I ever see anyone aiming at your back, I won't take time to invite him to turn around!"

He was kneeling by the body when Undersheriff Babcock came around the corner to exclaim. "Jesus H. Christ! Another one? Who was he, the one who fired that buffalo gun your way last night?"

Longarm indicated the fallen six-gun with the muzzle of his own as he soberly replied, "Not hardy. From that saddle he's sprawled across and the way he behaved yesterday, I'd say this one was a weak sister who'd decided to leave town, spotted me here betwixt him and his only way out without a mount, and Fred Waller yonder saved me from a back-shooting. But Russian Val, that Sharps .50-170, and at least one of the four men who held up Fred's post office are still around here *some* damned place!"

Chapter 20

The three dead bodies in Doc Maytag's cellar drew a considerable crowd to his drugstore. Meyer Levine confirmed that the bag of fancy imported licorice found on the last one had come from his creamery, but denied ever seeing the ugly cuss before.

The stagecoach crew were fairly sure the three men in the cellar had come south late in April with those recovered saddles. You tended to remember passengers who lashed saddles instead of regular baggage to the roof rails.

Dennis Phelan, their boss, said he'd never laid eyes on any of the sons of bitches before. That was one thing he and Merlin Oberon seemed able to agree about. So the bunch of them were allowed to resume their late start for the county seat, and Doc Maytag suggested Longarm and Undersheriff Babcock discuss the matter further over to the Chloride Saloon.

So that was where they were when the first wires started coming in.

The Texas Rangers wired that the surely identified Pecos Tim Sheehan had ridden with two pals on numerous occasions the state of Texas had been meaning to talk to them about. The one shot the day before over at Elvira Tenkiller's place added up to a wayward youth in his middle thirties known as Redbird Jennings. The sweet-toothed recent addition to the collection figured to be a bad apple called Candy Dawson. He'd been fighting a drinking problem with candy. The Rangers said they'd heard he'd lost his nerve since he hadn't been drinking as much.

Neither Emma Gould, Ruth Jacobs, nor the Women's House of Detention in Denver could offer any help with the mysterious Russian Val. But a wire from his Russian pals in Denver told Longarm of a serving wench called Tanya, Tanya Ivanov, who'd racked up a reputation for wildness on her nights off, before she'd been caught pawning church plate and lit out for parts unknown. When Longarm read she'd worked for the Deltorski family, he perked up to say, "I know them. I've been to supper at their handsome brownstone, and Sikorski's close enough to Deltorski when you need to make up a name to match your accent fast!"

Doc Maytag asked if, in that case, Longarm might have once been served by Russian Val in an unsusual manner indeed.

Undersheriff Babcock, who'd sprung for the scuttle of beer they were sharing at a corner table, laughed dirty and said, "Being served at a dinner table by a gal so famous for serving her rosy red rectum sounds unusual enough for me! What does she really look like, old son?"

Longarm replied, "Who looks at the hired help when you're at a fine dinner, hoping you won't pick up the wrong fork? I reckon I well *might* remember most anybody I saw setting at the table or serving the same, if I was to meet up with them tonight. But I can't say which of a whole herd of servants I might or might not remember this long after those dinner parties in a Russian neighborhood. I think our host, the Baron Deltorski, was holding forth on the Jewish question back in his old country. I ain't sure who was asking what about Russians of the Hebrew persuasian. But he seemed to think it was a hell of a question, and I do recall a mess of pretty young gals in sort of Gypsy costumes who kept serving up fish eggs and beet soup with gobs of sour cream, along with Russian tequila, which they call vodka. I wasn't invited to poke none of them pheasant gals in the ass, though. That's what Russian barons call their hired help, pheasants.''

Babcock asked if they'd wired anything about this Tanya Ivanov in Mulligan serving guests of Madame Velvet in another way.

Longarm said, ''They don't know where she ran off to after they'd caught her stealing. They were planning on sending her back to Russia. She'd been sent over here on some sort of indenture that didn't allow her to act up like that. They only know she ran off. But the description of Tanya Ivanov matches that of Russian Val. A petite brown-haired gal with brown eyes. Such a gal can look flashy or mousy, depending on what she wears and how she paints her face. If the same wayward gal is both Tanya Ivanov and Russian Val, a whole lot of mystery can be eliminated. If they're two different gals, nothing I've come up with works for shit!''

Babcock cocked an ear and said, ''Listen! Sounds like the volunteers are fixing to roll again!''

He got to his feet to bustle out the bat-wing doors, and Longarm followed at an easier pace. It was a local peace officer's job to worry about any breaches of the peace. Longarm was simply as interested as anyone else in clanging fire engines.

They joined the gathering crowd out front as the Mulligan Marvel Engine Company came along Main Street under a billowing trail of smoke. The engine, painted bright green with its brass fittings all agleam, was pulled by a dozen men in as many styles of dress. The coal-fired engine was meant to pump water, not move along the rutted street like a locomotive off its tracks, and a volunteer company that kept a team of draft horses curried, watered, and fed round the clock in a town the size of Mulligan was a prissy spendthrift outfit, not long for this world, where men were men and a man who volunteered as a firefighter was expected to show some grit.

So they loped on by with the upright boiler swaying perilously behind them as the big yellow wheels rumbled and grumbled.

It only took seconds for Longarm to make out where they were headed. The thick column of wood smoke had already risen a quarter mile against the cloudless cobalt sky. Madame Velvet's house of ill repute was on fire!

Longarm ran after the fire engine, along with most of the men and boys and some women as the alarm triangle went on ringing from the firehouse behind them.

Longarm came upon Portia Parkhurst, her saucer-eyed clients, and the two older servants out in Mine Road, where spilled water was already snaking along ruts and around horse apples as the Mulligan Marvel got to really pumping what looked like a futile stream of piss on a bonfire. It wasn't that their steam pump wasn't all that marvelous. The fire was just too ferocious, as all that weathered lead paint and well-seasoned pine lit up like a Hindu funeral pyre.

As Longarm joined them, Cordelia Gilliam told him in a childish tone of wonder, "Custis, our house is on fire!"

He said he'd noticed, and turned to Portia, who said, "It seems to be spontaneous combustion. There was nobody doing anything in the empty second-story room we think it started in. We were all downstairs, thank heavens, when old Gus there spotted the rising smoke as he was working in the garden."

Cordelia made a sudden break for the picket fence where it wasn't quite blocked by the engine company's sprawl of canvas hoses and other equipment. Her older sister, Cyn, had already grabbed her by the time Longarm and Portia could get to her. She went on struggling with the three of them, sobbing hysterically that she had to save the diary of Madame Velvet.

Cyn insisted, "Forget it, honey! You'd never make it up those stairs alive, and even if you could, every page will

160

be ablaze by now! Tell her, Custis! Tell her I'm right!''

Longarm got a gentle but better grip on the distraught Cordelia as he soberly said, ''That's likely what this fire is all about, Miss Cordelia. I see somebody's tossed a lot of baggage out into the yard. So it might not be as bad as it looks.''

Cordelia sobbed, ''What are you talking about? We've lost the house, and even worse, we've lost all those pages we've been counting on to make us really rich!''

Portia stepped in to shake her hysterical younger client good as she demanded, ''Snap out of it, you ninny. You and your sister should thank your lucky stars we're all alive! Mr. Oberon warned us all that there were powerful men who'd never stand for those pages and pages of pig-gish behavior to be published!''

The older sister, Cyn, chimed in with, ''*You* were the one who said something like this might *happen*, Cordie! I should have listened to you and just put the house up for sale while we had a house to sell.''

Cordelia sobbed, ''That was before all those editors you sent some pages to said they were doubtless worth a fortune to somebody braver!''

Cyn nodded wearily but said, ''Now that it's happened, I can't say I'm all that surprised or really upset. We still have the property there, and best of all, the two of us are still breathing.''

Portia caught Longarm's eye. He answered her unspoken question by saying, ''They might get enough for the cleared land to start over in the notions business back home in Wichita. Once it sinks in, I'm sure Miss Cordelia will see what a close call they had.''

Portia asked if he had any idea who it might have been.

Longarm asked, ''Would you like to list the likely sus-pects alphabetic or numeric, Miss Portia? You read what was recorded in the diary of Madame Velvet. Some of the upstairs adventures of now older and wiser men could strip them of their dignity at best, put them out on the street as

161

soon as an outraged wife could get to her lawyer, or even put a man in jail. There's no statute of limitations on some offenses, even when you commit 'em as a wild young drunk in a house of ill repute. You don't want to stand trial for manslaughter when the prosecution lawyers can prove you've enjoyed crimes against nature with the likes of Madame Velvet and her motley crew. But why am I telling *you* all this? You're the lawyer, not me!''

Portia sighed and said, ''Help me get these poor waifs over to the hotel. Their servants can follow with the baggage that's been salvaged once we know what's left here.''

Longarm turned to gaze about, until he spotted Undersheriff Babcock. He whistled, and when Babcock looked up, waved him on over. The older lawman hopscotched leaking hoses and wagon ruts overflowing with ink-black water until he'd joined them, staring up at the towering flames and declaring, ''That has to be arson. Who can we eliminate, pard?''

Longarm said, ''Let's eat this apple one bite at a time. If you'd be good enough to have these ladies escorted over to the Drover's Rest, I thought you'd like to back my play as I proceed to tidy up here in Mulligan.''

Babcock called out to some of his own deputies before he asked Longarm who they were fixing to arrest for starting such a fire.

Longarm said, ''I wasn't sent here from Denver to catch firebugs. I was sent here to catch the bunch who robbed your post office.''

Babcock chuckled fondly and said, ''Three out of four ain't bad. I take it you don't think that bunch had anything to do with this fire?''

Longarm said, ''Not directly. The only connection betwixt the late Madame Velvet and that post office job is that a former hooker of hers set it up. I was just now standing here, regretting the destruction of the diary of Madame Velvet, when it suddenly hit me why my pals in the Denver Russian community said there was a mighty wicked Russian gal at large in these parts, why riders who rode in these parts said there had been a wicked gal they knew as Russian Val because of her accent, and why the diary of Madame Velvet made no mention of her at all.''

By this time they'd been joined by half a dozen junior deputies. So Longarm said, ''I digress and time's a-wasting. I could use some backing if you'd care to tag along. There are two of them, with that Big Fifty buffalo gun between them, and Lord only knows who's the more dangerous of the pair.''

The older lawman issued curt instruction and tore after Longarm, who was already legging it up the road toward the mining company cabins scattered like children's blocks across the slopes.

As the undersheriff caught up, Longarm explained, ''I started out on the wrong foot. I had Russian Val doing their shopping and fronting for them whilst they lay low because at least one male member of the gang was too well known to risk showing his face in the daylight. I thought they were trying to kill me before I spotted *him*. They shit their britches and set out to kill me before I could get to town and recognize *her*, the play-pretty their leader was living with and doubtless enjoying to the hilt. They say she likes it up the ass, and lots of owlhoot riders go in for that sort of pleasure. It goes with spending all that time in jail or hiding out in lonesome cabins with other bad boys. Russian Val turned to a steady customer here in town when she got laid off as a whore. He used her for what stage magicians call *misdirection*. He had her act now and again as a scout, knowing we would sniff that red herring. He had his recruits from Texas convinced she was the brains and he was just another good old boy. In case they got caught. But he's been using *everybody*, the two-faced-no-good son of a bitch, and I'm so sore at myself for not seeing it sooner I could spit. It's all so simple as soon as you eliminate the ones it *couldn't* have been. But that goddamned diary of

Madame Velvet led my by the nose into one dead end after the other!''

He cut across the grain of the slope, surprising the older lawman as they began to swing downhill. But Babcock was an old hand at manhunting, so instead of asking dumb questions, he asked, ''Which company cabin are we approaching from the rear, old son?''

Longarm drew his .44-40 as they moved around an outhouse in a weed-grown backyard. So Babcock got his own six-gun out as Longarm strode to the back door and simply kicked it in without knocking.

The naked couple on the bedstead froze in the dog-style pose for a fraction of a second. Then the man who'd been sodomizing a grinning Russian Val, otherwise known as Tanya Ivanov, pulled his suddenly limp organ-grinder out of her ass and rolled off the bed to hit the floor and claw for the Big Fifty under the bed.

Longarm creased the bare rump of Russian Val to nail Fred Waller between the eyes as he came up with that lethal but clumsy .50-170. Russian Val sobbed, *''Nyet! Nyet!''* as she threw herself flat on her bare breasts and belly while her lord and master sprawled between bedstead and bloodspattered wall like a broken bare-ass puppet.

Undersheriff Babcock followed as Longarm stepped inside to firmly but not unkindly tell the trembling whore, ''He was right, Miss Tanya. Now that I see you in all that flesh, I do recall you from that dinner when you were waiting table for the Deltorski family. I remember how I admired your ass at the time, albeit not as much as that two-faced postal worker you've been giving it to. Don't it hurt? What do you and them pansy boys get out of having a dong up your ass like that?''

She didn't answer. She was bawling like a baby. Longarm let her. He knew from experience that once it sank in, she'd be proud to fill in all the details in hopes of saving her neck for her old age.

Undersheriff Babcock eased around the foot of the bed

to make sure before he said, "Jesus H. Christ. It was Ash Woodside's own assistant all the time! How did you ever figure that out, old son?"

To which Longarm modestly replied, "Eliminating, pard. Pure and simple process of eliminating."

Chapter 21

The undersheriff went to get help with the bodies, dead or alive. Longarm suggested the gal get dressed and at least run a comb through her hair, which in point of fact was a pleasant shade of brown—all over.

As she did so, she confided in her thick accent that she'd been a prisoner of the gang and that she was so grateful to him for saving her that she'd do most anything naughty or nice he might have in mind.

Longarm smiled thinly and warned her, "Try that defense in court and the prosecution's going to nail your feet to the floor and push you on your fibbing fanny, ma'am. A helpless prisoner ain't at all likely to sashay into a post office alone to see how crowded it is and buy a postal money order to make certain the postmaster opens that safe full of money on a busy day. A helpless prisoner ain't at all likely to approach a hotel clerk alone to see if a federal lawman who made it through her gang's ambush might be staying there. A helpless prisoner would have no call to suggest her captors kidnap another gal to find out what said lawman might have been saying about her gang."

He let that sink in as he stared down at her with his six-gun held politely. Then he said, "Looking on the bright side, you yourself ain't never really aimed a gun at anyone,

166

and in point of fact your lover boy and his Texas drifters have had mighty poor luck at killing others. So you might get off with less than five years in a federal prison, or for that matter, they might find it easier on the U.S. taxpayers, if harder on yourself, to just send you back to the Czar of All the Russians and let *him* figure out what to do with you.''

Her brown eyes got big as saucers and filled with tears.

Longarm said, "I figured you'd as soon do your time in an American penal institution. Would you like me to tell you how we might just work that out?"

She seemed to be calling him her "Dada," which sounded good enough. So Longarm said, "We call what I want you to do turning state's evidence. You can't hurt old Fred on the floor by giving away some of his little secrets this late in the game. But you might be doing yourself some good if I could hand you over to kindly old Judge Dickerson of the Denver District Court along with a full confession in writing and a waiver of your rights to a jury. Your average Colorado jury is more likely to throw the kitchen sink at a female furriner who steals church plate, takes it up the ass as a full-time whore, and interferes with the U.S. mails. So your best bet would be to throw yourself on the mercy of the court and take what Judge Dickerson shoves to you. Don't offer to be naughty or nice with him. He's more likely to want to shove a minimum sentence to you in exchange for helping us wrap a federal case up neat and tidy."

So she said in her comical accent that she followed his drift, and by the time Undersheriff Babcock got back up the slope with that buckboard, Longarm had cleared up the few loose ends that hadn't been plain to see before he'd headed up to Fred Waller's hired cabin.

At Longarm's suggestion they recruited the wives of two deputies and swore them in as Jefferson County matrons, so they could lock Russian Val or Tanya Ivanov safely away for the time being.

So then Doc Maytag had four bodies neatly lined up in his cellar with only the first one, Pecos Tim, starting to bloat a mite as the druggist cum deputy coroner declared his determination to wind up his infernal inquest before Longarm could dump another dead body in his lap.

Doc Maytag and his panel of seven found it just as comfortable as before to conduct the hearing at a corner table in the same Chloride Saloon. Longarm and Postmaster Woodside went along with the druggist because they knew he was only talking about the immediate causes of death. Events leading up to all four deaths were still a federal matter to be resolved more formally over in Denver, once more federal officers arrived to tidy up around Mulligan.

But Ash Woodside allowed that as long as they were jawing about the bullet in the brain of his trusted assistant, Fred Waller, he'd sure like to hear what had led Longarm to the sneaky young son of a bitch.

So, sitting across the table with a schooner of suds in front of him and a three-for-a-nickel cheroot gripped in his grin, Longarm explained. "It smelled like an inside job from the start. A roving band of owlhoot riders, out for a quick score, should have hit and run. I thought they *had*, to tell the truth. I wouldn't have known they were hanging around the scene of the crime like big-ass birds if they hadn't tried to ambush me before I could even get here."

He took a drag on his smoke and continued. "That was my first clue. The second followed as the night the day as soon as I considered how in thunder they knew I was coming. It wasn't on the front page of the *Rocky Mountain News*. I'd just been put on the case and gone to borrow ponies from personal pals on the outskirts of Denver. The only ones I'd told around the Denver Federal Building were the other federal men I worked with, and for all their faults I couldn't see any of *them* in cahoots with small-time holdup men. No offense, Ash."

The postmaster said, "None taken. I never said they'd robbed the Denver Mint. You figured somebody us government employees knew had been told, or overheard, you were coming. But Fred Waller wasn't the only cuss in town I'd confided in, and I don't think he'd ever met you. So how come he ordered Pecos Tim and Redbird out to head you off?''

Longarm said, ''It was Pecos Tim and Candy Dawson. He was the one who ate licorice. I made the mistake of assuming that Russian immigrant whore had been buying it for him. Fred Waller was running such errands as a more familiar face around town. His play-pretty was well known in Mulligan as a shady lady. So they kept her out of sight a lot, and she was the one they were afraid I'd recognize on sight. I did, the moment I saw her taking it in the ass. She'd served me fish eegs at a fancy brawl in the Russian quarter of Denver. When she told Waller this, he ordered me shot, not for being a lawman, but for being a lawman who, unlike the rest of you, no offense, could have spotted Russian Val from a furlong away in fair light.''

''But what put you on to Fred Waller if he had his gal and his pals hidden away out of sight by daylight?'' asked Undersheriff Babcock.

Longarm smiled sheepishly, took the cheroot from his mouth to wet it with some suds, and confessed, ''I really feel dumb about that. I took way too long. I let him sell me that notion he'd shot his last follower, Candy Dawson, to save my ass.''

Babcock said soothingly, ''It looked that way to me at the time, albeit now that I've seen the light, I'll bet Candy Dawson was losing his nerve and insisting on leaving town when the two-faced delivery man saw the chance to rid himself of a loose cannon. When they saw you there at the stage depot, Waller told Dawson you were there to arrest him and suggested he backshoot you whilst he had the chance!''

Doc Maytag marveled, ''The sneaky young bastard was *smart* too! He knew Dawson would never get away after gunning a lawman in broad-ass daylight without a horse to

169

call his own! So knowing Dawson was sure to be caught and made to talk either way, he backshot his own pal to silence him forever and make himself look good!''

''But what put you *on* to Waller?'' Babcock insisted.

Longarm said, ''The same thing that led me off down a false scent in the beginning. That diary of Madame Velvet never said your local post office clerk had been one of Russian Val's steady customers. It said he admired the Chinese delights served by some wild corn-holing whore called *Chop Suey Sally,* and I was looking for the friends of a famous *Russian Val.* I doubt the amazing Creole Annie was really a lady of color either. But I wasted a heap of brain cells trying to track such products of a vivid imagination, and I was really mixed up about a well-remembered Russian immigrant who never appeared in the diary of Madame Velvet at all!''

Doc Maytag asked, ''How come?''

Babcock explained it was a code, adding, ''She didn't want her star attractions serving time for going over the line betwixt good clean fun and downright disgusting. Ain't that right, Deputy Long?''

Longarm said, ''Sort of. I suspect the real intent was to shock her readers. As writ, that diary was intended to be published and curl the whiskers of many a prominent state and local bigwig. Since all of the names have gone up in smoke, I'll say no more about 'em, save for the fact that some important men indeed shared the favors of Chop Suey Sally and Creole Annie with lesser lights such as the late Fred Waller.''

Babcock said, ''I follow your drift! It's bad enough to be exposed as a married man who likes to get really dirty with a soiled dove. A respectable married man committing crimes agin' nature with a heathen Chinese or a nigger wench is likely to wind up neither respected nor married all that long!''

Longarm said, ''That's about the size of it. Mulling over that diary of Madame Velvet as I watched her whorehouse going up in smoke, along with all those pages and pages of tedious fornication, inspired me to suspect someone whose real name was in that diary might have set that blaze to make sure nobody ever read it there again.''

He stuck the cheroot back in his teeth and continued. ''That got me to more eliminating. Eliminating who could have done what over yonder and sorting out the names I recalled as making sense, side by side with those as didn't. Having established that all Madame Velvet's whores had been white and that Russian Val was a name everyone else agreed on, I figured Chop Suey Sally or Creole Annie had to stand for Russian Sally, and when I recalled having noticed with amusement that innocent young Fred Waller had spent lots of time up Chop Suey Sally's ass, it all fell in place as clear as crystal. Albeit I have to allow Russian Val herself just confessed to enough to make my official report hang together tidy as all get-out, once I turn it in along with her.''

He grinned with the cheroot gripped in his teeth at a jaunty angle as he added, ''Without her I'd have never known for certain how she'd met those three Texas drifters as a streetwalker around the Denver railroad yards, or how Fred Waller had been bitching about all that money in the post office safe, if only.''

A townsman came in to tell Longarm some ladies wanted him outside. He excused himself and followed the townsman to find Portia Parkhurst and the Gilliam sisters seated in a handsome open carriage drawn by four matched chestnuts. As he came over to tick his hat brim to the three of them, Portia indicated the young hands seated up ahead of them and explained, ''Mr. Flowers, the mine superintendent, has instructed these nice young men to drive us in to Denver. Gus and his wife will follow later, by coach, once they've salvaged what's left amid the ashes.''

The kid holding the ribbons said, ''We're driving the ladies in the short way, straight to the capital to catch their train, if they don't mind a few bumps along the way.''

Portia said, "I fear all that's left is the building lot, and I can take care of that transaction for them."

Cyn shot Longarm a roguish look and declared, "At least we still have our health. How are *you* getting back to Denver, Custis? You're welcome to ride in with us, and we don't have to catch our train back to Kansas right away."

Poor little Cordelia just sat there, wrapped in her own thoughts as her lips moved silently. From where Longarm was standing, it looked as if she was telling herself it wasn't supposed to have ended that way.

He said, "You ladies go on along and I may catch up later. I have to go up to the county seat at Golden before I return to Denver."

Portia said, "I know it sounds awkward, but wouldn't you save time if you rode with us to Denver and caught the narrow-gauge back out to Golden? You'd save more than a day. There won't be a northbound coach until the day after tomorrow!"

Longarm said, "I noticed. I wasn't planning to wait on any coach. I still have the stock borrowed from my pals at the Diamond K. They've been loafing around the livery here in Mulligan all this time. So they might as well earn some hay by loping me on up to Golden this afternoon."

Cyn Gilliam asked what was so important up in Golden, compared to a farewell supper with the bunch of them at the Denver Palace that same evening. Portia was blushing and glaring at him like a wet hen. He figured Cyn had bragged about him seducing her against her will in that pink bedstead. He hoped she'd really laid it on thick. Portia was more likely to doubt the sassy spinster if she gave him a few more inches than Portia might remember.

The kid holding the ribbons gently allowed it was time they got cracking if the ladies really expected to have supper in Denver at a resonable hour. So Longarm removed his Stetson and suggested they get going. He added that he'd call on Portia once he got back in to Denver his ownself.

Portia Parkhurst, Attorney at Law, said, "Don't bet on it! What business do you have up at the county seat to begin with? Weren't you here on a federal case and haven't you just wrapped it up in a manner I might have foreseen?"

He said, "Aw, they're always making a little gunplay into the Battle of Waterloo out our way. I have finished up here in Mulligan. So now I'm riding up to Golden to make another arrest."

"To arrest whom, on what charge?" asked the born lawyer despite her annoyance with him.

Longarm said, "I aim to arrest the one who set fire to the estate of the late Madame Velvet, of course. Before you cloud up and rain all over me, I know arson ain't a federal offense, Miss Portia. I ain't going after the cuss for setting fire to the house of any . . . friends."

He wound up with the hat in his hand to say, "The charge is murder and filing false federal mining claims," before he whipped the rump of the nearest carriage horse with his hat and added, "See you back in Denver, if I win." And then they were off in a cloud of dust as he put his hat back on and grumbled, "I sure wish they hadn't told old Portia. But what the hell, old Elvira Tenkiller ought to still be up around Golden, and *she* ain't sore at me worth mention!"

Chapter 22

They made it up to Golden before sundown, starting late after more damned forms to sign in Mulligan than you could shake a stick at. He made certain the Diamond K stock was in good hands at the Golden livery, and then he went and had a set-down supper of steak and potatoes with two slices of fresh-baked carrot cake for dessert before he tried to find out where Elvira might be staying.

Nobody he talked to knew. But it kept him busy during the supper hours, and so sure enough, when he ambled over to the Lookout Saloon, Lookout Mountain being the name of the considerable rise just west of Golden, he found old Dennis Phalen engaged in a game of five-card stud in the back room with some other local swells.

As Longarm entered what was supposed to be a private gathering, the coach line owner glanced up in annoyance. Then he smiled and called out, "The news proceeded you by telegraph wire. You made our evening edition and how come you're so mean?"

He waved expansively and said, "Boys, I want you all to say howdy to the one and original Longarm. The one who just shot all those holdup men down in Mulligan."

He smiled up wisfully to add, "I missed that last one you got the minute our backs were turned this morning.

What are you doing up this way, seeing you've accounted for all four of them and arrested their doxy?"

Longarm said, "Come up to Golden to make another arrest. You are under arrest, Mr. Phalen, or whomsoever you may really be."

It got very still in the back room of the Lookout Saloon, with the only sounds the scrape of chair legs moving back from the table as the man known as Dennis Phalen stared thoughtfully up from behind his iron-gray beard, whether smiling or not.

Then Phelan quietly asked, "Have you been smoking that Mexican weed, Deputy Long? Just what loco charge did you have in mind this evening, and do you have any idea who you're talking to?"

Longarm said, "Nope. I'm working on that. You and the diary of the late Madame Velvet put you in Georgetown, over by Silver Plume, in the year of Our Lord 1867."

The older man looked relieved and said, "Aw, shit. You can't arrest a man at this late date for showing off atop the bar with a double-jointed little thing who, all right, might have been sort of young to be working in a whorehouse."

One of the other men rose to declare, "I don't have a dog in this fight, gents. So if it's all the same with all concerned, I'll just be on my way now!"

Nobody stopped him. Two others followed him, leaving Longarm there with the stage-line owner and a consumptive cuss who looked as if he was fixing to pass out under his pearl-gray Stetson. Longarm stared thoughtfully at the unknown quantity and murmured, "*Bueno,* any number can play and your first mistake, posing as a customer of a younger Madame Velvet out Georgetown way, was that you couldn't seem to remember that famous saloon sign. It was as if someone in years to come were to say he'd gotten his start here in Golden but couldn't remember any Lookout Mountain or that Coors draft every saloon in Golden seems to have on tap."

The bearded plutocrat in the expensive brocaded vest

shrugged and said, "So I was in town to get laid. It was years ago. I just thought something up to get that pansy Oberon out of my ear. What kind of a name is Oberon anyway? Wasn't Oberon the king of the fairies in that tale by Shakespeare?"

Longarm nodded and said, "Dennis Phalen would be an Irish name. You don't talk like an Irishman, Mr. Phalen. You talk like a New England Yankee and you're known to be a tight man with a tip. Yet the Dennis Phalen Madame Velvet recalled from the Georgetown boom was a generous broth of a boyo before they heard he'd struck it rich and sold his claim for a fortune to a big mining syndicate. A mining syndicate made up of accountants, engineers, and other dry sorts who'd never met up with the *real* Dennis Phalen at Madame Velvet's—and don't try that, you asshole!"

But the burly bearded man's manicured right hand kept going for something under that brocaded vest. So Longarm fired first into the gun hand to Phalen's right, and then into Phalen himself with the second round of his double derringer.

As the lean consumptive shootist let go of the gun in his lap to follow it to the floor sideways, the portly killer in the expensive vest clutched at the vest where his blood was coming out in spurts, and asked in a surprisingly conversational voice, "How did you do that and who told you?"

Longarm dropped the little smoking whore-pistol in a side pocket of his frock coat, and reached under the coat to get out his more serious .44-40 as he calmly replied, "It's generally a good notion to have a weapon in hand as you walk in on a killer's card game. As to who told me, *you* did. I had nothing but suspicions until you made your play to get rid of that old diary, lest somebody read it and come to the same conclusions I had. We sort suspects out according to motive, means, and opportunity. Plenty of men had *motives* for wanting them scribbles suppressed. You were the only one who'd managed to get an invite allowing you free range of the property. Nobody else on the premises had been named in the diary of Madame Velvet. How did you do it? Lit candle burning in a pile of kindling in one of them deserted rooms whilst you left town with time, as well as houses of ill repute and dirty writing, to burn?''

The man pretending to be the long-dead Dennis Phalen didn't answer. Longarm stepped closer, waved his fingers in front of the bearded man's staring eyes, and muttered, ''All right. Don't tell me. Let me guess!''

The two muffled gunshots from the back room had naturally not gone unnoticed, and Longarm was glad he'd thought to pin his badge on when some other lawmen charged in, guns drawn, to demand some damned explanations about the deaths of two such prominent citizens.

So it was too late to ride back to the Diamond K by the time he'd filled out even more infernal depositions, and he got a room in the Castle Rock Hotel near the narrow-gauge terminal instead.

Thus he was stretched out on the bed in his underwear, reading a paperback copy of *Honest Harry, or the Country Boy Adrift in the City,* by C. Norris, when there came a hesitant rapping on the hall door.

Hoping old Elvira had learned he was in town, but ready for worse, Longarm drew his six-gun from its holster against the bedpost and rose to glide over on the balls of his bare feet and open up to, of all people, Portia Parkhurst, Attorney at Law.

She looked around from her fight-or-flee stance in the doorway to observe, ''I see you're alone tonight. Don't know any women in Golden, eh?''

He calmly replied, ''As a matter of fact I do. But unlike some I could mention, I don't pester members of the opposite sex late at night. Are you coming in or staying out yonder? I'll look like a total fool standing here like this if somebody comes out to see what all this late-night chatter is about!''

She grudgingly followed him inside. As he shut the door,

she told him, "I ran into that typist from your office. Not Miss Bubbles. That pallid youth called Henry. The typist you haven't slept with, or have you?"

Longarm quietly replied, "You'd best leave now, Miss Portia. I ain't never heard Henry low-rate you, and I'll not have you low-rate him to me."

She said, "Oh, don't be so proddy. When Henry told me about you getting into another gunfight out here in Golden, I hopped the narrow-gauge in case you needed a lawyer. They told me over at the sheriff's department that you'd solved a perfect crime. I guess I should have gone right back to Denver, but how did you solve a perfect crime, you clever thing?"

Longarm moved toward the bed to put his six-gun away as he told her in a matter-of-fact tone, "You don't. A crime is only perfect until somebody suspects it's been committed. I got the state police working on just who the man we knew as Dennis Phalen and his skinny sidekick really were. He was bidding on that empty house of ill repute just to find out whether Madame Velvet had mentioned the real Dennis Phalen in her notorious diary. When that literary agent, Oberon, allowed he'd admired a lusty young Irishman who could impress wicked ladies with his unnatural virile member, the fake Dennis Phalen knew he had to make sure no such record of the real Dennis Phalen existed."

Longarm sat down to continue. "Neither man is now alive for us to question in detail. But the cuss pretending to be Dennis Phelan had grown up speaking English in the New England way, and the county coroner just assured us he had an average . . . build. He may or may not have looked enough like an Irish immigrant with no American kin to matter. He only had to kill the real Dennis Phelan to sell his claim to gents who'd never met either, and then simply stay away from anywhere the real Dennis Phalen might be remembered."

Portia blinked and recalled, "But Dennis Phelan *had*

been remembered, in detail in the diary of Madame Velvet!''

Longarm nodded and said, ''I noticed. I'd noticed a lot of things in them pages and pages that had me chasing my own tail like a pup. For a whole lot of cutting and splicing had been going on, making room for stuff that had never been there so's a lot of stuff that Madame Velvet had never writ could be slipped in for local color. That's what you call made-up crap like the romance betwixt James Butler Hickok and Miss Calamity Jane Cannary, local color. A lawman trying to resolve Hickok's death in the Number Ten Saloon by reading he'd been screwing a professional drunk could get confused as all get-out. So . . .''

The lawyer settling the accounts of the late Madame Velvet cut in. ''Back up. You're going too fast! Are you intimating the diary of Madame Velvet wasn't really written by Madame Velvet?''

Longarm nodded wearily and confessed, ''I sure felt stupid when it finally hit me. For once I saw I couldn't have been reading what I'd thought I'd been reading, everything started falling in place like a row of lined-up dominoes, see?''

Portia shook her head and demanded, ''If those pages and pages of sordid confessions weren't the diary of Madame Velvet, what were they?''

Longarm answered without hesitation, ''A mighty ambitious forgery. I had to do some eliminating before I could be certain. But there were a few things about them pages and pages that rubbed me wrong right off. I had to wonder why anyone so devoted to gardening never mentioned a single spring planting in records going back eighteen years. I had to wonder why most of her customers over the years rated little more than an observation that so and so had paid such and such for this or that, whilst others who'd go on to be famous in the *future* of a particular volume rated whole purple passages about their perverse pleasures.''

Portia frowned thoughtfully and decided, ''I can't see

how anyone back in pioneer times could have had such foresight either. Now that you point it out, I could kick myself for not having noticed that!''

Longarm said, ''Another thing that bothered me was the simple law of gravity. Why would anyone who had a family home she visited regular go traipsing all over the mountainous mining country of Colorado with them heavy twenty-four volumes, counting the blank spares? Wouldn't it have made more sense to store the sins of yesteryear with her kin in Kansas and read them over on trips home if need be? I suspect the originals must have read more like dirty but dull business ledgers before someone with more imagination saw an old whore who'd been ailing wasn't really leaving her heirs anything anybody else would care about. For as that literary agent warned, you can't just sell tedious lists of names as the confessions of a female Casanova. So she buckled down to rewrite the whole nineteen volumes as a seamless effort in the same handwriting, and I hope it gave her writer's cramp. For she had me all confounded with her mishmash of truth and falsehood.''

Portia said, ''Good Lord, it must have taken anyone else months, if not years, to rewrite all those volumes!''

Longarm nodded soberly and said, ''That's what had me confounded. I could only think of one way to produce all them pages with nary a page replaced in factory bindings and every infernal page written in that same schoolgirlish handwriting. Once I'd caught more than one passage that just couldn't have been written by the real Madame Velvet, I had to consider *others* who'd had the motive, means, and opportunity. Nobody but the Gilliam sisters fit that pattern, and Cordelia fit it best. But I just couldn't picture that coy young thing taking on such a laborious as well as dirty job, until it came to me, staring up at all that smoke as their inherited house and everything in it, that nothing *else* would work at *all*. I still can't see brassy Cyn concentrating long enough to write one naughty love letter. So it had to be shy little Cordelia who rewrote the diary, destroyed any original

180

volumes on hand, back home or out here, to let her brassy sister discover the family treasure and do all the talking. I admit I'm guessing at some details. But there's no other way on earth those nineteen volumes could have been rewrit as an almost undetectable forgery.''

Portia stamped a foot and demanded, ''Stop teasing me and tell me how you knew it was a forgery if you found it such a great job!''

Longarm shrugged and said, ''All I had to *know* was that it *had* to be. Everything fell in place at that fire, whilst I was standing there like a big-ass bird, picturing all nineteen volumes of fancy wood-pulp paper, crisping black a page at a time to blow away as white ashes in the wind. That was when it hit me that you couldn't *buy* wood-pulp paper anywhere in the U.S. of A. nineteen years ago! I'd forgot, and I reckon Cordelia never read that article in the *Scientific American*. But they'd assured us the first American paper mill grinding wood-pulp for paper was built after the war, around 1867 or so. I could have asked the shy thing when she sent away for a new mail-order set that matched her old aunt's originals fairly close, but she seemed so upset after watching all her toil and trouble going up in smoke, I felt no call to upset her any further.''

Portia sniffed, ''How merciful! You know damned well you compromised yourself as the arresting officer no matter *which* of them did it, and honestly, you brute, was there any woman connected with the case you didn't have your wicked way with, aside from me, that is?''

Longarm calmly replied, ''I never met Madame Velvet and I never felt a thing for Russian Val. That's all I have to say about my wicked ways, and if you feel left out you have nobody to blame but yourself.''

''I know,'' sighed Portia Parkhurst, Attorney at Law, as she snuffed the lamp to undress in the dark, laughing like a mean little kid.

Watch for

**LONGARM AND THE FOUR CORNERS
GANG**

252nd novel in the exciting LONGARM series
from Jove

Coming in November!

Explore the exciting Old West with one of the men who made it wild!

JAKE LOGAN
TODAY'S HOTTEST ACTION WESTERN!

J. R. ROBERTS
THE GUNSMITH